Prodigal Son
By
David Allen Kivi Jr.

Cover by Kyle Kedzuch

For Mom and Dad, they always believed in me.

Prologue

Theo Bokan looked over the soon-to-be Capital city with pride. The young man was tall, with broad shoulders; he sported dark hair that reached past his shoulders but was kept in a ponytail that jutted from the back of his head but left the rest of his hair free. He wore a fancy shirt and this new thing called a vest, along with brown pants and his regular boots. He left his signature sword and dagger in his room (there was no more need to be armed just walking around anymore). Many of the buildings were still being constructed. Along with the Imperial throne—well, the soon-to-be Empire of Stone's crowning glory. Called the Black Stone Spire, hundreds of Dwarves from the East had come to help make the obsidian stone tower. They were using every trick that they knew, and were creating several new ones to make the impressive structure. Years of his hard work, years of constant war and chaos were coming to an end, the Empire would provide safety and security for years to come and he couldn't be happier about the part he played in it.

Well, he *could* be happier and the reason why landed behind him. Theo turned around on the roof of his soon-to-also-be finished estate to the see the Matron of his family standing before him. She had pale skin and hair that shimmered silver in the morning light. Her sharp, blue eyes seemed to bore into his very soul, the way only one of her kind could. He bowed deeply to the beautiful woman before him.

"Matron, I had not expected you today," Theo told her as he stood up from his bow. She seemed to ignore him as she walked past to look over the city as he was just doing.

"So, this will be the shrine to your folly?" she asked, her voice light but deep with wisdom. Theo suppressed his deep sigh as he turned to stand next to her.

"This will be the seat of the Emperor's throne, yes," he told her, not hiding the pride in his voice.

"Theo. You are too smart for this! I taught you better than this!" she replied, not bothering to look at him.

"Is this not what you wished us to accomplish? To use the gifts of the Judicators to do this very thing, provide a safe and peaceful place for all peoples of any race and religion?" he asked without anger, but more concern that he had angered her instead.

"I gave your elders my gifts so that they might fight for a better tomorrow, and be prepared for the future, not to relinquish your powers on the hope that everything would be fine," Matron explained before sighing loudly. "I doubt I can convince you to give up this foolishness."

"I am sorry, Matron, but I feel this is for the best," Theo explained confidently before he bowed his head at her. She sighed again before taking off into the air, flying into a cloud and out of sight. Theo couldn't help but feel as if he had betrayed her, but he knew in his heart that this course of action was the best for everyone. In the world he was crafting there would no longer be a need for individuals like him.

The first morning bell rang out over the city and Theo nodded his head as if to agree to the morning itself. He finished getting ready, including these new garments called coats; although he kept his cloak handy, these coats were more fitting. Theo was about to leave but strapped his sword to his waist before leaving, knowing he wouldn't need it, but after years of wearing and using it he didn't quite feel right without it. Theo left his estate and walked down the new stone streets to the Black Stone Spire. Guards, soldiers he had served with in battle, bowed as he approached the Palace. Theo smiled at them as they righted themselves and bowed in turn to them. They all had a chuckle; he was never one for the pleasantries for nobles. He patted them on the shoulder in turn before entering.

He was ushered into the throne room like the great hero he was. The throne room was huge, carved out of the black rock only ever found in the West. The new Emperor's throne was itself carved from the stone, and ground smooth, not impressive at all, but it suited the room well. All the banners from those families that had sworn fealty to the new Emperor hung on the walls. The Bokan family banner hung there as well: the griffin flying in front of the blazing sun sewed on a scarlet flag. The room was filled with all manner of people: Men, Elves, Dwarves, Halflings and Gnomes from all distant lands. Theo just smiled and shook hands and said hello when prompted. Several servants were handing out glasses of wine. Theo took one and pretended to drink as he walked to his family's banner, running his fingers along the edge. The flag was a gift for his grandfather and now he couldn't think of a better place to see it hang.

"Theo Bokan!" He heard a voice call behind him, and Theo turned to see a large man in full-plate armor come marching up. The man was very tall and his head was shaved to the skin, and a large great-ax strapped on his back. The man had a big blonde beard and looked him over with sharp hazel eyes.

"Callous de Bloom!" Theo called back as he rushed to give his longtime friend a hug. The big man picked up Theo and hugged him tightly. "Easy, you'll crack a rib!" Theo exclaimed as his friend laughed before putting him down. Theo regarded him for a moment as he caught his breath and leaned a hand on Callous before continuing. "How are you, Vindicator?"

Callous scuffed at him with a throaty growl. "What about you, Judicator? How are you?" Theo scuffed right back at him, and Callous gave a throaty chuckle. "So this is it, huh? Fancy parties and drinking wine the rest of your life?" he asked, gesturing to the glass.

"Better than dying on some godforsaken dirt field full of dead bodies and blood, my friend," Theo told him a knowing smile, and Callous nodded his head.

"Hey, I hear the Lords and Ladies of the Seasons will be here," Callous stated boldly to Theo's surprise.

Theo looked puzzled for a moment. "The Seasons aren't ones to bend knee to anyone."

Callous shrugged at his friend. "I think it is more of an alliance than bowing before Thelus, to be honest," he responded and Theo agreed with him.

"How did I know I would find you two by yourselves?" Maclin Hamiltin came up to them. The man wore a tricone hat with a sliver pin on the left side and a long, light gray greatcoat with golden stripes sewn into the left sleeve. Maclin was a grizzled older man with a salt-and-pepper gray beard and hair. He wore nicer clothes under his coat and carried a rune sword, forged by the Dwarven blacksmiths.

"Maclin, how are you?" Callous asked, slapping the man on his shoulder.

"Getting old," he replied after he rotated his shoulder. Theo chuckled at the exchange.

"Other than that, how goes it being the first Inquisitor?" Theo inquired of the older man.

"You know, finding the truth behind the lies, bringing fairness and justice to trials...It's very trying some days." Maclin looked old and frail for a moment as he sighed deeply. Theo understood, more than perhaps anyone.

"Maybe one day we will no longer need Inquisitors; that one day we have finally achieved an Empire founded on truth and justice that will no longer need our kind." Theo stated and Maclin smiled for a moment. The blow of horns alerted everyone in the room that Thelus, the soon-to-be Emperor, had arrived. Everyone kneeled in turn as the Elf entered the room.

Thelus was very tall, even for an Elf. He had light golden hair that was long and flowing under his sliver circlet. He wore a set of elaborate robes the color of pure white snow, with sharp green embroidering in ancient Elfish words. His bright yellow eyes looked around the room and he smiled as he approached the center of the room.

"My friends," he began, his voice booming through the room. It was a strong and powerful voice; a voice that had moved mountains and brought even bitter rivals to an end and shook hands with friends time and again. "Please stand. This is a day to celebrate proudly standing among our friends and allies, not kneeling before a tyrant." The room laughed as they stood up. "I know we have all been through a lot together—fought over a hundred battlefields, scoured our would-be enemies to the four winds." He paused, his eyes saddening some before continuing. "And we've lost friends." The room was silent. "We lost brothers and sisters, fathers and mothers. Lovers and better halves...Some of us have even lost children during our struggles."

"To those lost but never truly gone!" Theo shouted, raising his glass high. The nobles raised their glasses, while the warriors raised their fists and shouted. Thelus raised his own glass and nodded to Theo before they took a drink from their glasses.

"Often it takes the word of a Judicator to help me remember what we have accomplished, rather then what we have lost," Thelus declared to the room and they seemed to agree as he walked to Theo. The crowd parted as he approached them. "Theo Bokan, the greatest Judicator of our time. When I had the idea to bring peace and order to this land, Theo's father, Levin, was the first man to pledge his support to my ideas. Theo was a just a boy when his father rode off to war with me time and time again. Theo was barely in his teens when Levin had to return on his shield, instead of riding by my side." Thelus placed his hand on Theo's shoulder. "I was proud to call him my friend, and I am just as proud to have his son fight with me. Never has another Judicator come across my path with as much conviction and honor as Theo Bokan. I was proud to call him my friend, and I am just as proud to have his son fight with me. Never has another Judicator come across my path with as much conviction and honor as Theo Bokan here."

"Here, here!" Callous shouted, clapping loudly. The room joined in cheering along with him. Thelus smiled brightly again as he squeezed Theo's shoulder.

"None of us would be here without the dedication of the Judicators and Vindicators. With all of your help and support, we forge a new Empire: one that I will see provides a brighter, safer future for us all. One were we will not lose friends and loved ones to senseless, constant war and strife!" Thelus roared happily and Theo joined in with the cheering.

He knew he had made the right choice. The time of the Judicators was over—it was the time for the Empire of Stone now.

Chapter 1-
Five thousand years later...

The sun crested over the mountains, and the light of the first rays of the dawn touched the outlying desert city. The sandstone buildings were almost pale in the morning light. The golden dome over the local temple glinted and shone into Jacques' face. He opened one eye and immediately regretted it. Turning over in his bed, he muffled his groan against a pillow. It would be hot soon, and even though he was naked it wouldn't help him remain cool. Jac signed loudly as he stretched his back and his arms, then brushed his dark brown hair out of his face. He then felt a soft female body brush against him, and he smiled.

Melda, one of the local Belladonna Maidens, was with him. Belladonnas were an organized group of mistresses and escorts for hire. They would undergo years of training to learn to please their clients, and it was even rumored that they were spies and sometimes assassins for the Empire nobility. Jac smirked at the idea; he knew they had their own political agendas but that was as far as it went. He felt Melda's soft, supple breasts against his skin and grinned. They had spent at least four nights out of the week making love. The young Elven girl had taken him by surprise; it was almost a year ago now when Jac was making his visit with the Madam and she introduced herself without provocation. She was a local girl by birth, reflected in the dark skin tones and darker, thick hair of many of the natives in the area. As with all Elves, she had long, pointy ears that allowed her exceptional hearing.

This side of the Empire of Stone was hot, sandy, and a bunch of bullshit. Jacques had been sent here to see to his family's holding as owners and operators of many of the Empire's weapon factories. One was located here in Muzrun. The Dwarves had settled in the mountains long ago and created Muzrun to do business with traders going through the mountain pass to reach the countries Klac and Mondor respectively. The factory here was one for guns and pistols as the Empire had discovered the technology some years ago and had been at work improving it ever since. Repeating pistols had been the newest thing. With a magazine for six to eight rounds that could be fired before the weapon had to be reloaded, it had changed the face of warfare. As the Emperor commanded that the Orcs and Goblins of the west would be pacified or destroyed as the Empire expanded into the frontier.

Jacques couldn't be bothered to give a shit, honestly. It was the poor man's job to fight and die for the Emperor, not his. It was more or less his *devil-may-care* attitude that has gotten him in trouble. James, his father, had been embarrassed rather publicly a few times by Jac and had sent him off to this pit of hot, sandy despair about two years ago now. Jac was either to learn his lesson or wait out his father retiring from running the family and leave it to Jac, as the only son in the family. Jac had a sister, Ioney, who he missed terribly just about everyday, and on the very rare occasion he had been allowed back home he spent much of his time with her.

The rest was generally spent with Harrison, his best friend since they were children. Harrison de Bloom was the head of an equally important and wealthy family, much like Jacques', although Harrison had mostly kept out of trouble while Jac had dragged him into it. Still, they were very close and tried to talk as often as they could. Jac was seriously missing his sister and friend today.

He grumbled loudly at the thoughts that went through his head this morning. His situation was not changing anytime soon. Before his thoughts could over take him again, Jac felt Melda's soft lips kissing his neck.

"You're awfully whiny this morning." She spoke softly, just like the rest of her.

"Sorry, I was just thinking," he told her and she made noise.

"Handsome boys aren't allowed to think, I keep telling you that," she replied as she got on top of him and they kissed tenderly. Her delicate skin was cool against his and soon he was raised and ready for her, and before Jac knew it they were back at it. He wasn't sure about his feelings for Melda. She was great, and they talked as much as they were physical and she seemed to genuinely like him for being himself. Jac could have gotten himself another Belladonna at any other point in the last year, but Melda made him feel good in more ways then one.

All too soon, though, they had finished and Jac had washed and gotten dressed. With the hot weather he usually wore loose trousers that wrapped a silk sash around his waist and stomach and wore a loose vest. Jac walked into the morning sun and wished he had purchased a hat at some point, or a cloak, but after a minute or two his eyes adjusted. Muzrun was very big city. While much of the city was in the desert that butted up against the mountains, most of the Dwarves lived in the mountains themselves. He had to walk through the local bazaar to get to the factory, which he didn't mind. The smells of exotic spices and fruits filled the hot air, and no matter how many times he strolled through the area he still enjoyed all the smells, although he would give a whole lot of coins for a green apple, which of course he indulged in every time he was home.

Jac bought his usual spicy curry and some goat cheese, along with a mug of Grendor coffee. The black, bitter drink always kicked him awake in the morning; apparently the country was mountains, hills and valleys, all lush and fertile. Traders around here could make or break their reputations on the quality of coffee beans they brought back. Jac took his usual seat by the bazaar's fountain to eat his food and drink his coffee. He enjoyed watching the hustle as humans, Dwarfs, Elves, and occasional Halfling or Gnome came through and traded with the locals. As the overseer for the factory, Jac was allowed a generous allowance, and since he stayed on the property owned by his family he had few expenses.

Of course, he also had increased the factory's production twofold since he arrived, as he had sacked the lazy manager and found one worth his salt. That led to more profits, which lead Jac to a higher allowance. Jac may have been in exile from his home, sister, and friends, but he lived comfortably.

Jacques finished his breakfast and one of the local runners came up to him. The little boy picked up his dishes and Jac tossed him a gold coin, ten times what the service was worth.

"Thank you, Mr. Bokan." The small boy smiled widely at him.

"Just don't spend it all on sweets," Jac told him and messed up the boy's hair, and the boy ran off to return the dishes to the vendors he had bought the food from. Of course the food vendors paid them or kept them fed, too, but Jac was more then happy to spend his father's coin. He was about to get up and make his way to factory finally, but newcomers to the market stopped him dead: three of them, all wearing tricorner hats and black long coats of Imperial Inquisitors. Each wielded a rune blade that could cut through armor like paper and a repeating pistol. Every Inquisitor was deadly with those weapons and carried the weight of the Empire with them. If they felt the need, they could have you and your family dragged off if they thought you were a threat to the Emperor. There were two men and one woman. He had seen the men before: they were from the local office of Inquisitors, but the woman was new. She had bright red hair and fair skin, more akin to people like him from the capital.

She spotted him and smiled warmly as she approached, Jac stood up and bowed to her; it was always in your best interest to show respect to an Inquisitor. Especially when they smiled at you, it much like a Warg smiling at a Goblin—there was bound to be teeth and blood soon.

"Good morrow, Mr. Bokan. A lovely morning, is it not?" she asked after he stood from his bow.

"Yes, it seems to be a pleasant one today, but as soon as the sun is a little higher in the sky you might wish you weren't wearing that big coat," Jac explained trying to joke with her. She chuckled slightly and nodded her head.

"I believe you are true in your words, but there are many secrets that we Inquisitors hold. Keeping cool in the desert is one of them, I am afraid," she told him and Jac seemed impressed that she was so open to him. "I am Inquisitor Kesh Calmor. I have heard many things about you."

"All good things, I hope," Jac stated with a worried smile. An Inquisitor who knew you was hardly ever a good sign.

"Let's just say it's of the mixed variety."

"Ah, I see."

Kesh chuckled again. "Just stay out of trouble, Jacques, and we'll be on good terms."

"Of course, Inquisitor Calmor."

"Please, just Kesh for the time being. I am sure I'll be seeing you around town."

"I am sure you will," Jac told her as he bowed slightly, and she raised her hand. Jac placed a tender kiss on the back of her hand and she turned back toward her fellows. Was she flirting with him? That could be a great sign, or a terrible one, but Jac didn't have time to decide: he needed to head toward the factory.

The huge wooden building stuck out like a sore thumb against the background of the other sandstone buildings. The large smelter in the back of the building gave it two large chimneys that blenched black smoke into the air. The factory was built here because of the metal mines that the Dwarves had worked in for over ten thousand years. Over two hundred Dwarf and human craftsmen worked here for eight hours a day. Jac came in through the main office doors, and Nada, the receptionist, smiled at him as he entered. She tended to wear silk, almost see-through pants and the same kind of top that covered her chest and arms.

Her hair was always in a ponytail that fell down her back, with numerous beads of gold, sliver, and a few other gems woven in. Appearance was everything to the customers who came in to order weapons, and this factory was the finest on the east side of the Empire. Plus, it took little convincing on her part for Jac to buy her new clothes or jewelry; not only was she very tasty eye candy, but it also meant spending more of his father's money, something he had very few problems doing.

"Good morning, Jacques. You are a bit later then usual," Nada admonished. Jac shrugged his shoulders.

"Had a rather interesting encounter with an Inquisitor this morning. I'm not sure if she was trying to get me to confess to wrongdoing, or get in my pants," Jac explained as he picked up the papers Nada handed to him.

"Well, I know from experience that your pants are very loose." She smiled wickedly; another reason Jac had no problem buying her pretty things.

"I suppose we will just have to see." Jac brushed his hand across her face, to which she blushed slightly as he walked toward his office.

It couldn't have been more then an hour before Jac was bored. He lazily flipped through the production papers and everything appeared to be on schedule for their next big order. No clients were scheduled for a meeting for at least a week and there wasn't even anyone to yell at. So when his manager, a Dwarf named Graz, came in, Jacques thanked whatever gods he could think of for the distraction.

"Morning, boy!" Graz, blunt as usual, one of the many reasons Jac liked the older Dwarf and hired him for the job. The Dwarf was about average size for his kind, with a long salt-and-pepper gray beard that was braided into his belt buckle, which depicted a leering demon face. Otherwise he was in a simple shirt with a leather apron that also covered his pants.

"Morning, Graz! How's work this hot, boring morning?" Jac half-asked, half-whined at him. Graz scuffed and waved him off.

"It's tough being the boss, ain't it?" Graz asked and laughed.

"You remember this when I am running my family's estate and I make you the boss."

"Pfft, I don't care for idle threats, boy!" This time they both laughed. Jac did really enjoy the older Dwarf's company a lot. "Come with me to the workshop, got something for ya." Jac didn't think twice or question the other man; anything to get him out of his office.

They walked across the factory floor, and most of the workers waved or smiled as they passed. Jac had seen to it that his workers were fed while they were at the factory, which of course cut into the profits, but increased production and worker happiness. Jacques was well known in town for running a productive business but with happy workers. Half of the people here were hired by him as his father wanted to expand the factory—especially the workshop, where craftsmen came from as far as the frontier to work for him.

Graz was a skilled craftsmen as one could find was not surprised when he had taken over a corner of the workshops for his own projects. A number of different plans lined the walls and scattered parts and pieces covered the tables along with tools, many of which were a mystery to Jac.

"Now, where did it go?" Graz began moving things from one table to another, in a vain attempt to find whatever he was looking for. "Blast it to all the Thirteen Hells, where is that box?" Jacques chuckled to himself as he began looking around for a box. He spotted a length of cloth covering something box-shaped.

"Is this it?" Jac pinched a corner of the cloth and was about to pull it off when Graz turned to look.

"Yes, now hold your boars, boy. It's a surprise." Graz slapped his hand away. Jac could help but laugh a little. Graz loved surprises, more then any Dwarf he had ever met. "Now, this is one of a kind, my boy." Graz turned around and held a wooden box that was engraved with Dwarven runes. He opened it up and showed Jacques the most beautiful gun he had ever seen.

Graz cleared his throat before he spoke. "This is a Gunderman special, an eight-shot repeating pistol. I inscribed runes so it will always fire straight and true, never misfire, and will never break. It's a standard breach loader with a removed clip, to which I made two spares. It will take any standard size shot for its size and can even take rune shot."

Jac looked at him, a little puzzled; rune shot was what mages used in their weapons. "I'm not a mage, Graz," he explained and Dwarf brushed it off.

"I know that, lad, but I am just saying that this kind of pistol can fire just about any type of bullet you have on hand. It's a fine weapon for one such as yourself. I even had a leather worker made a holster and bandoleer for ya. I figure if you ever need a pistol if you decide to go hunting or anything, I'd be proud if you wore this."

Jacques smiled at his friend. "I would be very proud to wear this, Graz. This is finest weapon I've ever seen, thank you. I don't know how to begin to pay you back." Jac picked up the gun from the case. It was balanced and sighted for him, and it felt light but was very solid. Jac noticed Graz's craftsmen symbol on the butt of the grip. The hammer breaking a rock had graced many things, and now it graced one of the finest weapons ever made.

"Just remember me when you are back in the capital, my boy, that's all I ask."

Jac slapped him on the shoulder. "How could I ever forget?"

Chapter 2-

The midday bell rang through out the city and Jac told Nada he was going home for a bit during lunch and left Graz in charge. He carried the pistol, still in its box, along with the holster over his shoulder and a pouch full of standard shot for the weapon. The street was a clustered as it usually was for this time of day as people were out looking for something to eat. The sun was high in the cloudless sky and for the second time today, Jac wished he had a hat of some kind.

A raven cawed overhead and Jac looked up to see the black bird flying just overhead. It landed on a windowsill and cawed again at him, very loudly. Jac was puzzled why the bird was so far into the desert. After a moment it fluttered and took flight, past Jac and into the sky. He followed the bird with his eyes as it flew away but it was gone before he had a chance to really see it. Jac looked back down and shook his head and happened to spy down a side alley. A gang of local thugs seemed to be gathered there. Then Jacques saw why they were gathered there.

A young-looking girl was being tossed in between them; her blouse was torn at the shoulder and she was crying. Jac took a step forward and then stopped himself to think for a moment. He looked down the street and the little boy from the morning was running around with a few other kids. Jac whistled loudly and caught the boy's attention.

"Yes, sir, do you have more dishes for me to run?" the cheerful boy asked as he approached Jac.

"No, but I do need your help." Jac handed him the box and boy clearly struggled holding onto it. Jac opened the box and pulled out the weapon and broke open the gun and began loading it. "I have two gold coins for you. First, I need to you hold to that box with your life, you understand?" The small boy nodded his head. "Okay, the second is that I need you to run and grab any of the town guard you can find and bring them here, understand?" He nodded again, Jac handed him a coin, and then the boy ran off. Jac took a deep breath and spun the clip around before swing and slamming the gun closed. He holstered the weapon before walking up to the thugs.

"You know," Jacques declared loudly and the group turned around to look at him. "This is really the wrong way to ask a girl out."

"Beat it, rich boy." One of the bigger thugs came walking up to him. "Or we might see how much gold comes out while we pound on you."

"Wow, I've got to say, that is the stupidest thing I've heard in a really long time," Jac replied sarcastically. The larger man gritted his teeth as he pulled out a dagger and lunged for Jac. Without thinking, Jac drew the gun in such a way that he knocked the blade out of the thug's hand and pressed the gun barrel under the other man's chin. Everyone was surprised, even Jac, although he managed to hide it well. "Back off, dung-for-brains, before we find out just how little of those you have." The large man held his hands up and took several steps back. Jacques held his hand out for the girl and she came running behind him.

"We won't forget this, pretty boy." The leader of the group spoke up, and Jac stepped up and aimed the gun at him.

"Want to test me, goon?" Jacques asked him pointedly but no one spoke up. "That's what I thought." The terrified girl was clinging to him as they walked backwards out of the alley and back into the street. It was a good few blocks before Jac put his pistol away. "Well, that was exciting." He smiled at the girl, who just burst into tears and clung to him. "Hey, it's okay now, I've got you. Let's go find some help." The girl nodded into his shoulder and Jac walked with her down another block before he saw the boy he told to get help.

Four of the towns guard had him surrounded. One was holding the box that Graz gave him another one was holding the boy off the ground as he was kicking and the other two were looking through the boy's pouch.

"Where did you get this?" one guard asked.

"I bet he stole it; he looks like a thief to me," the second one said as he produced two of the gold coins Jac had given him.

"What in the Thirteen Hells are you doing?" Jacques shouted at them as he lost his temper. The girl had let go of him and taken a step back. "I sent his boy for help and you are treating him like a criminal?" The closest guard turned to stop him.

"This is none of your concern; move along, citizen," he told Jac but Jac just pushed past him.

"Do you have any idea who I am? I can see the lot of you thrown into the desert for this!" Jac was shouting at this point.

"I said *get*!" The guard tried to grab him but quicker than Jac could think he had pulled his pistol out and had it pressed against the man's forehead.

"Do you have any idea what you're doing?" the first guard asked.

"Putting some more scum in its place? Yes, yes, I do..." Jac glared at the guard as they were about to unsheathe their weapons, but before things could get out of hand someone cleared their throat pointedly.

The group turned to see Inquisitor Calmor consoling the crying girl. "You best do as the man says, or I will throw you out in the desert, if you survive the fall off a guard tower first." She spoke with authority and guards begrudgingly let the boy go and he snatched the coins away from them. Jac ripped the box from the first guard's hands and they leered at each other for a time. "I believe you have other places to be, and you can consider that an order." They left without further problems and Kesh sighed heavily. "Damn locals," she said under her breath. He noticed the boy had a cut on his lip that was bleeding.

"What happened?" he asked the little boy.

"One of them knocked me down when I came running. I thought they were the helpful kind of guards, but I guess I was wrong," the boy explained and Jac shook his head slightly.

"What's your name?"

"Balin, sir."

"Okay, Balin, stay right here and I'll see to it that we get you patched up," Jacques told him. "Thanks for that, it could have ended very badly."

"See, *this*," she said, waving her free hand around in circle to make her point more, "is what I am talking about when I say 'staying out of trouble.'"

"This was not my fault, this time," Jac replied and Kesh smirked at him.

"Well, thankfully you saved this girl from gods know what, and for that you have my thanks. But I am afraid you all will have to come down to the Inquisitor's Office and explain what exactly happened here," she told them and motioned in the general direction.

"Of course, I want nothing more then to get my side of the story on record."

Chapter 3-

It took much of the afternoon, but Jacques explained in great detail the events that transpired after he left the factory. Jac was sitting in Kesh's office, waiting to see the outcome of the events. Kesh walked in and handed him a glass of water. She had removed her hat and long coat, as well as her sword, which was hanging on a hook near the door. Her red hair seemed to look brighter, but Jac wasn't sure if it was the lighting or her hat that made it look darker.

"Figured you might be a bit thirsty." Kesh sipped at her own glass. "We are just finishing with the girl. It seems she is the daughter of a tavern owner; she went out for bread and was cornered by these goons. I am afraid to say that we have yet to find the group in question, though."

"So this is the part were you tell me I should probably hire a bodyguard or two and be careful for a few days?" Jac replied. He had heard this speech a few times already.

"We both know your past, Jac. I would say that it couldn't hurt. I hear you like to spend your father's coin like it was going out of style." Jac chuckled to himself.

"I wouldn't even know what is in style these days. It's been way too long since I've been home at the capital," Jac told her, and Kesh nodded her head to the right.

"Yes, I do believe your current attire would be a bit chilly this time of year," Kesh joked with him as she sat the edge of her desk. She set down her glass and motioned to Jacques' pistol. "May I?" she asked respectfully. Jac nodded his head and pulled the gun out of his holster. She handled the weapon carefully, as though it was made of glass. "This is a beautiful weapon."

"Thank you. It was a gift from my manager, and he is quite the craftsman. I'm glad it came in handy today." She seemed to nod as she handed the weapon back to him.

"Thank your gods when you return home; surely they have smiled at you to-day."

"Indeed," Jac stated as he holstered his weapon.

"Well, I honestly don't see a reason to keep you any longer then I already have," Kesh told him as they both stood together. "I just should mention that the boy, Balin, he doesn't have parents. I had our medic take a look at him and other than his busted lip and being a little underfed he seems to be fine. I would understand if you want me to send him to children's home." Jac was a little taken aback by the information but he shook his head.

"Ah, no, I'll, um...I'll see to him," Jacques said, surprising both of them.

"Very well then. If we do catch the gang members, I would ask you to identify them for us."

"Yes, of course. I am sure you can find my family's estate, and the factory. I'm not really one for the night life out here."

"Why should you be? You have a live in Belladonna." Jac was taken off-guard by her comment but just nodded and headed out the door.

Jacques had gathered up the boy and headed to his home. Melda was waiting in the front sitting room. Once he was through the door she rushed to him, embracing him sharply.

"I was so scared when I heard you were in the Inquisitor's office," Melda said in between kisses. Jac smiled as he pulled her off of him and held her at arm's length.

"I'm fine. I was there because I helped a girl today. I promise, Mel, that everything is fine." She smiled widely at him and peered around to see the little orphan behind him.

"Hello," Melda said as she crouched down to look him in the face. Balin smiled brightly before he replied.

"Hi! You're very pretty." Melda chuckled a little.

"Thank you," she replied warmly.

"This is Balin. He helped me out I owe him. I figure we could feed him and give him a good night's sleep at least." Jac told her and she wore a warm smile he had rarely seen with her. It wasn't one of lust, which he usually saw, but something different, like she knew a secret no one else did.

"Well, I am sure I can find something for my heroes," Melda said as she rose, and took Balin's hand and lead him through the house.

Later, after feeding Balin and tucking him into one of the guest beds, Jac and Melda were in the master suite. The sun had passed below the horizon, and the night bell had already rung. A cool breeze blew through the town, chilling the night a bit. Jacques was looking over the dark night, till he felt Melda's soft hands wrap around him and she pressed her cool body against his.

"I thought I told you this morning, pretty boys aren't allowed to think," she told him softly.

"How can you tell I was thinking?" Jacques asked, not bothering to turn his view.

"You wear this longing look on your face and stare off in the distance. That and you moan a lot when you are doing it in the morning." Jac chuckled with her; she made a very valid point. "What are you planning to do with Balin? He is a very sweet boy, for one living on the streets."

"Swept you off your feet already, has he?" Jac smiled and turned his head to see her behind him, and she slapped him in the chest. "I'm not sure. I don't know why I agreed to take him. When Kesh said he was an orphan I just thought that I couldn't let him rot in a work home or anything. I suppose I'll see about making him a ward of my family and give the boy a chance, at least." Jac turned and embraced Melda again. She looked him in the eye and they kissed softly.

"Despite your tough skin, you have a very dear heart, Jacques. One of the reasons I love you." Jac looked surprised at her.

Jac looked at her, surprised. "You love me?" Jac asked, a bit stunned, but she just smiled her sweet smile and nodded before they kissed again.

"Do you love me?" she asked. Jac couldn't get a read on her, but he nodded his head yes.

"Yes, I do." Jacques smiled at her and this time they kissed with passion and fire.

"Take me to bed," Melda whispered into his ear, and he was all too happy to oblige.

This morning Jacques was up before the sun. He sat up against the headboard of the large bed. He was partly watching Melda's sleeping form; her naked body looked supple and inviting but he had other things on his mind. When the sun crested the mountains he looked out the window again. Had he really said he loved her last night? Had she said it back to him? Or was it just some kind of strange dream?

Jacques searched his feelings thoroughly and was still unsure of what he was feeling. It wasn't lust, that was for sure, he knew what that felt like; in great quantities, mind you. No, this feeling was surely something new and different. It could be love. Jac couldn't recall a time he felt like he was in love, but then again he had never felt this way about a woman before. Of course he was completely unsure of what to do now. His family had expectations and that generally meant that he would have to marry into another family and bring strong ties to his. An Elf Belladonna was not exactly the ideal wife to bring home to his family.

Melda stirred next to him, and when she opened her eyes she looked up and smiled at him.

"Good morning," she whispered and Jac almost couldn't believe what came out of his mouth next.

"Good morning, love." This made her smile brighter. He slipped down farther into bed with her and began to kiss her in earnest. Suddenly the front bell rang—someone was at the door. They pulled apart and looked at one another. "Who could be here at his hour?" Jac asked out loud, not exactly at her. He rose out of bed and searched for his trousers. Melda pointed toward the balcony, where they were hanging off the stone railing. He quickly grabbed them and put them on as she chuckled at him and found a robe for herself.

Jac made his way to the front of the house as he quickly tied off the attached sash, and poked his head into Balin's current room. The small boy was still sleeping soundly. Jac closed his door quietly as the bell rang again and he shuddered involuntarily. Jac made his way, finally, to the door and was rather surprised when he opened it.

Kesh Calmor was standing there patiently, with her hands behind her back. Jac was a little lost for words.

"Um, Inquisitor, what do I owe the pleasure? Found the thugs from yesterday?" Jac asked and Kesh shook her head.

"Afraid not. There is a call for you at the town hall." This was a surprise.

"I didn't know the phone lines were finished this far from the capital."

"Apparently they have been for sometime now, though there just wasn't a need for any kind of calls just yet. But I believe your sister is looking for you."

"Ioney has called me? What for?"

Kesh shrugged her shoulders. "That, I am afraid, I do not know. I was simply at the town hall for Inquisitor business and the morning runners had yet to show up. So I offered to deliver the message myself."

Suddenly Melda was behind Jac and he turned when he felt her approach. She bowed with Elven grace at Kesh.

"Inquisitor," Melda spoke just above a whisper and did not make eye contact.

Kesh tipped her hat to her. "Ms. Sandwind," she stated politely. "That is all currently. If the news brings you back to the capital, I would like to be informed so I can adjust my investigation accordingly, please."

"Of course, thank you, Kesh," Jac said and Kesh simply cocked her head to the side and tipped her hat again and walked off. Melda waited for Jac to close the door before speaking.

"On first name basis with an Inquisitor? Have you gone mad?" she asked, anger flooding her voice as it rose a little.

"Relax, she introduced herself the other day and helped me out a few hours later. And she just came to deliver a message to me. I have to find some clothes. My sister has called me from the capital."

"That can wait. Tell me all about her."

Jac took a stern stance with her. "Melda, I will explain everything, in great detail, but later. My sister called and I need to found out why."

"Promise me!" She was almost shouting, and Balin stumbled into the room. He rubbed one eye sleepily.

"What's happening?" he asked, half asleep. Jacques turned and smiled at the boy.

"Nothing important. Why don't you wait in the kitchen and I am sure Melda will come and help find you some food in a moment."

"Okay," was all he said before wandering back into the house. Jac turned back to Melda and held her shoulders as he looked into her eyes.

"I promise," he told her. She just regarded him for a moment before taking a deep breath and nodding. "I love you," he told her out of nowhere.

"I love you, too." Jac kissed her before rushing up stairs to put on a loose shirt, and with a second thought grabbed the holster and pistol. He checked and made sure the weapon was fully loaded and that the bandoleer was full of bullets, too. Jac then rushed out the door without any further words. He walked briskly to the town hall. It had been over seven months since Jac was back at the capital and had seen his sister.

The town hall was the biggest building and was the tallest, with the town's bell atop the tower. It had stood almost unchanged for over three hundred years. The wooden telephone poles that reached from the hall up and over the mountains had changed the landscape a bit. Jac had almost forgotten all the technology that was missed this far out. A number of Dwarf guards patrolled the building and the accompanying grounds and gardens. The Imperial Magistrate's office was here and handful of Imperial Regulars were milling about, as well.

Jacques walked through the front doors and to the receptionist's desk. Two Dwarf ladies were moving papers about. "Hello, I'm Jacques—" he began.

"Bokan," one of the ladies cut him off. "We've been expecting you, sir. If you'll come with me, the only working phone we have so far is in the Magistrate's office." She walked around the counter and off into the building. Jac followed her easily, as Dwarves were not known for their speed. "The Magistrate is not in yet but we have sent a runner to explain the situation to him. I am sure you will not be distributed but please do not take up his office for too long; he is not known for his patience."

"Yes, unfortunately I've met the man," Jac replied as they walked and the woman snickered. Jac had met him a few times for the two years he had been on exile: first when he took over the factory and another when the factory was expanded. Both times left a sour taste in his mouth. Jacques was used to leeches as it just went along with being in a noble family, but the Magistrate was lower than those people. An angry and ill-tempered little man with a taste for the finer things, Jac had wondered if he was here because he was forced out of the capital, too.

As soon as the office door was closed Jac sat down in one of the guest chairs as he picked up the receiver.

"Um, hello?" Jac spoke hesitantly.

"Jac!" He heard his sister's voice and was relieved to hear her after all these months. "I didn't wake you, did I?" Ioney asked, a bit unsure. She always worried too much about him.

"No, for a change I was actually up already, but the call does come as a bit of a surprise."

"Yes, I can understand that; usually I am more than happy to send a letter, but this is too important." She paused for a long time, and Jac wasn't sure she was still there until she spoke again. "Father, has...Father has passed away..."

Chapter 4-

Jacques walked out of the office a bit numb. He stood at the front desk in a haze for a moment. "Mr. Bokan, can we help you?" the other receptionist asked, coming up to him. He shook his head and cleared the fog that seemed to have seeped in after the conversation.

"Ah, yes, yes...I need a train ticket to the Capital. When is the next train leaving?" Jacques asked, trying hard to focus.

"The next train leaves tomorrow, at noon. I can have a ticket sent to you in the morning, if you wish?" she asked kindly but with some worry in her voice.

"Yes, that will be fine, thank you." Jac smiled as he walked out into the street. Out of all the things he expected to hear from his sister, that was certainly the last thing. Jac wandered around and before he knew it, he was standing in front of the factory. Graz happened to be there and was opening the front door.

"Jac, boy, what are ya doing here so early in ta morning?" Graz asked, concerned. This was certainly out of character for him.

"My sister called me. My father passed away, three days ago." Graz looked surprised and took Jac's arm.

"Come, lad, let's sit 'e down and get ya a stiff drink," Graz told him as he pulled Jac through the factory and into his office in the workshops. Graz plopped him down in a chair and produced two mugs and a bottle of amber liquid from his desk. "Always keep a spare bottle, my pappy would say. And by the great stone ancestors, was he ever right about that." Graz poured the liquor into the mugs and handed one to Jac, who took it out of reflex.

Jac stared at the mug for a long time before he finally drank it down. The liquor burned his throat and made his eyes water. "Bah! What is this?"

"The finest Dwarven whiskey that will ever grace your dull human taste buds. Now, tell me, what happened?" Jac shrugged his shoulders. Ioney had been pretty brief over the phone and he still wasn't quite sure what really happened.

"I guess my father fell ill since the last I've been gone, and he just slipped away," Jac told the older Dwarf, who just nodded grimly.

"So what'll ya do now?" the Dwarf asked, surprising Jac a bit, as he wasn't even sure. He was more than ready to leave Muzrun just a few days ago, but now...

"Well, I have to go home for the funeral and sort everything out, I suppose," Jac explained.

"Aye, lad."

"I'll need you to keep things going for a while, till I have things figured out."

"Of course, lad; I'll keep this place going like a well-oiled machine."

"Thank you, Graz. I've got to go home and get packing."

"You take care, lad, and go bury your pappy." They shook hands as Jacques headed out of the factory. Jac walked back to his home and stood there for a moment before he walked in. Melda was sitting with Balin, wearing a deep purple dress he had bought her a few months back. She paused and looked up and Jac was fairly sure she was about to yell at him but stopped when she took a look at him.

"Balin, sweetie, why don't run to the market and get us some bread for dinner tonight." She handed him a coin and he smiled before he ran off. Melda stood up and walked up to him; they didn't say a word between each other. Melda simply put her arms around his neck and pulled him closer. Jac pulled her into him and felt tears running down his face.

The train station was underground in the mountains, as the Dwarves had cut it out of the stone. The room itself was massive, larger than the town, with several air vents cut throughout the rock to let the smoke from the trains to escape. Melda was wearing a more conservative dress that mostly covered everything. She had one of the other maidens watch Balin while they went to the station.

"Here." Jac handed her a large purse, which jingled, full of coins. "I took out all the money I had at the banks here. It should be more than enough for you two while I am away." Melda had never handled so much coin before. "Once everything is said and done I will send for you. So keep enough to get two train tickets to the capital."

"I doubt your family will be thrilled when your whore just shows up," Melda told him, a bit harshly.

"Well, they can get over it. I finally found what I want in life. I wasn't lying when I told you I love you."

"And I love you, but what will we do then?"

"We'll figure it out, but I promise I will move heaven and earth for us to be together." Jacques lifted up her chin and they kissed. He looked deeply into her eyes as they parted. "I promise, we'll be together." She smiled at him then and he hated that he would ever have to leave her. "I'll send for you as soon as I can."

"Okay," Melda replied, simply but sweetly, and they kissed again. Jac smirked at her before he headed off to the train platform. Jac handed his bags to one of the stewards and then his ticket to one of the takers.

"Ah, yes, Mr. Bokan, you have a shared cabin," the taker stated.

"Um, no. Excuse me, I believe I purchased a single cabin," Jac stated, a bit puzzled.

"Well, actually, sir, your ticket says 'shared cabin.' I am afraid we are booked full." Jac sighed heavily but waved his hand for the taker to lead him to his cabin. They made their way through the train. Thankfully the cabin was spacious enough for two with a curtain that came down the middle and the bench pulled out into a small bed, big enough for one. He plopped down on the seat, which was very comfortable, and waited for the train to start moving.

There was a soft knock at the door and then the door slid open gently. A very lovely woman came walking in, wearing a full dress that laced up to her neck. She also wore a pointed cap with a feather sticking out from the front. Jac rose from his seat as she smiled at him. A steward was carrying a small case for her.

"You can just set that down, I'll be fine, thank you." She had a lovely voice with an accent from beyond the Empire. She handed a gold coin to the man, who smiled politely and walked off. "You must be my cabin mate for this journey."

"Ah, yes, I am Jacques Bokan, Ms. ...?"

"Ms. Blanch." She did a little bow, which gave away the fact that she was from Bocha, a nation of islands far past the desert. The Shiplords of Bocha kept a tight hold of transpiration and shipping throughout the islands. "I have heard of you, Mr. Bokan. You saved a poor girl from some hooligans."

"Well, that traveled fast," Jac stated and Ms. Blanch giggled slightly.

"I am sorry, gossip is one of my faults," she apologized before she sat down. "I hope you will not find me intrusive, but why are you heading to the capital of your Empire?"

Jacques sat down after her and took a heavy breath. "My father has passed away, and I need to take care of family business, I am afraid."

"Oh, I am sorry to hear that. I hope it does not bring any ill will towards me?"

"No, not at all, just has not quite sunk in yet." She smiled and nodded to him before producing a book from her bag and began to read quietly and left Jacques to his thoughts.

Chapter 5-

In the Black Stone Spire, the Imperial Palace, and main headquarters to the Office of Inquisitors, Rodrigo Sheld walked through its halls to the Inquisitor Supremes' Office. Jasmine O'Thoun had been an Inquisitor longer then Rodrigo had been alive. Although he was quite the up-and-comer, so to speak, Jasmine had demolished whole rebellions and executed hundreds, if not thousands, of rebels in her lifelong duty to the Empire. Most Inquisitors were picked from the orphan homes and workhouses from the toughest of children, or the smartest who happened to escape. Rodrigo managed to beat a boy six years older than him into unconsciousness and before he knew it he was learning to be an Inquisitor.

He had no idea why he was walking in their most hallowed halls, but when he spotted his immediate superior being dragged out with a knife in his chest, Rodrigo suddenly had a better idea. He composed himself before knocking on the door.

"Come in!" a strong female voice shouted from the other side. Rodrigo opened the door and entered the office. It was smaller than he would have thought, but still had a number of things made of gold, along with a large portrait of the Emperor behind the high-backed chair. Jasmine, the Halfling Inquisitor, was busy filling out papers. She looked up with bright purple eyes and had a raised eyebrow. "And who the hell are you?"

"Um, Inquisitor Rodrigo Sheld, ma'am. You called for me?" Rodrigo asked, a little puzzled and the senior kept looking at him.

"And why do I care, or, better question, why shouldn't I just kill you for barging in my office?" Rodrigo stuttered.

"Um, well, ah." Jasmine continued to watch him flounder for minute before she burst out into a roar's laughter.

"Of course I know why you are here! Rodrigo, please sit." He let out a sigh of relief before looking at both chairs. "I must apologize—it is in my nature to joke a little from time to time." One of the chairs was covered with blood and she noticed as well. "Oh, yes, you probably want to sit in the other one. Your supervisor decided to be more incompetent then usual and paid the final price for it."

"Yes, I saw that on the way in. I suppose I will be taking over his case?" he asked, still looking over the blood-drenched chair.

"Yes, I have already put his resources under you. Now you must understand this," Jasmine stated and Rodrigo looked back at her. "This may be the single most important case of your career, and accomplishing this will earn you glory and respect until well after you are long since dead and gone." Rodrigo raised one eyebrow; he knew better than to speak or ask questions when his superior was on a rant. "The Bokan family has been a pillar of the Empire since almost the very beginning. They own and operate several weapon and armor plants, and provide over half the equipment to the many brave men and women of the Imperial Armies.

"So when I say this, it does come with a certain sadness. James Bokan is a traitor to the Empire and paid the price as such. Now I need the full fury of the Office of Inquisitors to bear down on the Bokan family and find out just how far this corruption runs—if it is just his close family or all of his family or worse. Your former somehow managed to expose James, but slipped up and got his informant killed, so expect to dig deep here."

"And once I find just how far this goes, I am to cut the infection out, of course," Rodrigo quoted from his lessons as an Inquisitor.

"No, only fire can free the Empire of this cancer. I want you to burn it all out, burn it till there is nothing left to burn."

Jac sat on the train, in his shared cabin, as the train rumbled down the tracks. Ms. Blanch, his companion during this trip, sat quietly reading. Before Jacques knew it, the tunnels had given way to the open air and the train rolled over the mountains and then down into Chance's Forest. The trees were a blur as the train ran through woodlands, broken up every so often by the guardhouses that protected the train tracks from the threats in the forest.

Jac remembered going hunting a few times with his father and uncle before his uncle was called to the frontier. He remembered sitting near a forest clearing and lining up the perfect shot on a buck, but the buck had stared at him and Jac found that he could not pull the trigger. His uncle, Gavin, had patted him on the shoulder then.

"Don't worry about it. If it doesn't feel right then don't take the shot." Gavin smiled at him as if he couldn't be prouder and Jac remembered feeling good then. He also wondered if Gavin would be coming to the funeral or if he couldn't get away from the frontier at all. Jacques couldn't remember the last time he had seen his uncle. Probably when he was still a child. He remembered being really sad when he had to leave. *"Always be true to who you are, Jackie boy; never let anyone else define who you are."* These were Gavin's parting words, and Jac had promised his uncle that he would always be himself and never let anyone try to shape the man we was going to be.

Suddenly the trees darkened and Jacques caught himself in the reflection of the glass. His hair was grown out and a mess. His skin was tan from the desert sun and his eyes were dark from the lack of sleep the night before. He hardly recognized himself; he wondered how Ioney or Harrison or his mother would view him now. Now his mother he was looking forward to see, but with a grain of salt, though. She had always lectured him about his non-noble ways, but had been more caring at times. Suddenly Jac was aware that someone was speaking to him.

Jacques shook his head clear and looked over at Ms. Blanch, who was speaking to him. "I apologize, Ms. Blanch. I was lost in my thoughts."

The pretty woman just smiled at him. "It's understandable; I was simply asking if you'd like to accompany me to the dining car. I get very lonely on these trips and could use some noble company, much like yourself." She smiled brightly, disarming Jac quite a bit.

"I will, of course, be grateful to dine with you, Ms. Blanch, but I am just unsure of how much good conversion I can supply today," Jacques explained.

"Trust me: on these trips anyone is better than no one," Ms. Blanch joked with him and Jac felt himself smile a little, the first time in two days.

"Then, by all means, let's brood together."

Chapter 6-

Dinner was actually pretty pleasant between them, Jac being more upbeat than he thought he would be. They came back to their cabin still joking a bit.

"Then Harrison has the poor girl around her arms and he looks at me with this blank stare. And I ask him what happened, and he just says, 'I don't know. First thing we were laughing and drinking, next thing she was passed out in my groin.'" They both laughed hard and Ms. Blanch slapped him on the arm.

"Mr. Bokan, you are just the worst," she told him as she walked into the cabin.

"Yes, but at least my imposed exile has tempered my rowdiness quite a bit."

"I'd usually say that would make the case worse, but you seem to have gone on to improve yourself."

"Well, I did that for me, just to piss my father off. Just to prove to him I could do it, and better than he could. Of course, that didn't stop me from spending his money, but I made him more than I ever spent."

"It seems to have aged you a bit." Ms. Blanch suddenly realized what she said. "I mean in a good way, as though you've grown wiser."

"It's fine, truly. I've been called much worse," Jac told her with a bit of a chuckle. They both seemed to pause and stare at each other.

"Julia." Jac looked at her, puzzled. "That's my name. Please feel free to call me just Julia."

"Jacques, but my friends call me Jac most of the time," Jac replied and she smiled at him.

"Well, I suppose we should get some sleep; it is getting late."

"Yes, I am sure I have a busy few days a head of me." Jac reached up for the curtain and began to pull it down.

"Good night, Jac," Julia stated before he finished.

"Good night, Julia." He smiled at her and finished pulling the curtain down.

The train stopped at the main station for the capital. The vast city center stretched out before him. Towers and buildings reached to the heavens, smoke poured from chimneys, and the sound was almost deafening from the sheer rush of people. Giant gears turned all over the place, along with clockwork men that moved from place to place, preforming a number of different duties. A jet board-ers' gang flew up and overhead, followed by a squad of Imperial Slicers on their flying boards. The light metal boards had twin engines that let the board soar through the air, with foot controls to help turn the board or give it more speed. Imperial Slicers were in a crescent moon shape with two large engines that al-lowed speed and stability, but boarders were a reckless bunch and tended to mod-ify the boards to be faster and more dangerous. An Angel wearing the purist of white dresses stood on a high ledge looking down at all the people, her wings spread out behind her, shimmering in the morning light. Then at the center of the city lay the capital, the giant Black Stone Spire, the Imperial Palace itself. Thou-sands of Dwarves had worked day and night for almost a decade to complete the monument to the Empire.

Jacques helped Julia off the train and they got their luggage together, al-though Jac had only a backpack and case while Julia had quite a bit more. He slung one of the bigger cases over his back while one of the coach hands met up with her and started to carry some of it, too, but it still left Julia carrying two bags by herself. They reached her coach and Jacques helped the coachman load every-thing.

"Well, sadly this is where we part ways, Jacques," Julia told him as they fin-ished loading everything.

"Indeed. I am afraid so," Jac replied with a bit of a smile.

"I hope our paths cross again soon. You are very pleasurable company."

"I hope that as well." Julia held out her hand and Jac laid a kiss on the back of her hand. "Safe travels and happy health, my lady." He watched as she entered the coach and was off to her family's estates. After a moment, Jac put his great coat on. It was cold here, away from the desert. He heard a raven call above him, and Jacques looked up at the bird with puzzlement. It called two more times and flew away. He shook his head after the bird left; it was not the first bird he had seen, nor would it be the last.

Jacques walked over to the coach station and hired a driver for the rest of the day. His first stop was Harrison's office. Always the modern one, Harrison had his main office in a building of a new stone they were calling concrete. It was attached to the family's old, red brick warehouse. Jacques walked in, unannounced, after convincing his assistant not to say anything.

Harrison was about his height with sandy blonde hair he kept short, and his piercing grey eyes had stared Jac down more times than he could count. He wore the latest style of white dress shirt and green tie, with a green vest with the chain for a pocket watch. He looked quite surprised to see him.

"Jac, what in the Hells are you doing here?" he asked as he got up and closed the door.

"Good to see you too, buddy," Jac said as Harrison paused and sighed.

"Yes, sorry." They had a friendly hug very quickly. "But you can't be here—there's a warrant out for you."

"What?" Jac asked, very surprised.

"I sent men to the train station after I found out about it. Your father told me he was in trouble over a month ago, and he suddenly he got sick. The Empire got to him and now I am trying to cover our tracks," Harrison explained as he went to the wall and pulled on a candle holder. The wall slid open and Jac followed Harrison into a tunnel.

"'Our tracks'? Harrison, what is going on?" Jacques demanded, and Harrison sighed as they walked down the tunnel.

"Listen: your grandfather found out about some of the Empire's secrets and told your father, who told me. Our families have far more in common than just nobility," Harrison told him as they reached a secret office. Books and tomes lined the walls, and a map of the known world was on the table with a lot of different pieces scattered across it. "There are numerous forces in the world, and sadly the Empire of Stone, the one we have pledged our lives to, has been lying to us the whole time." He pulled a small book out from one of the shelves. "Look, I don't have a lot of time to explain everything. Just know that I am trying to get everyone out of this hole." Jac pocketed the book, his head spinning. His father was a traitor and his best friend was in on it.

"Now, Jac, I need you to follow this path and take it to a warehouse, and then I need you to wait for my people to come and get you. They will smuggle you out of the city, but you have to wait."

"What about my sister and mother?" Jac asked, suddenly worried about them.

"I am working on getting them out, too, but so far as I can tell my contacts say it's just you and your father they wanted. I don't know if his sudden passing was the Empire or what happened, but our plans hinge on you, Jacques."

He looked at his friend, confused. "What do you mean, our entire plans hinge on me? Hinge on me doing *what*?" Harrison stopped and looked at Jac, as though he was seeing him in a whole new light.

"We had power, our families, all of our families, we had power..." Harrison stated angrily, then shook his head as if to throw it off his head. "Look, Jac, I am truly sorry, but you have to go. This all works if I don't get caught." He pulled a book off the shelf and the bookcase swung open to another hallway. He was almost pushing the stunned Jac through the door. "Remember: wait for my people and I will get your sister and mother out of the city."

"Thanks, Harry, I'll owe you," Jacques told him and Harrison smiled at him.

"If things go the way I want them to, I'll owe you, my friend. Now go. I'll be missed before long," he told him as he closed the door and Jac walked down the corridor. It came to an abrupt end with a metal ladder leading. He took the ladder up and found himself in an empty warehouse. Boxes and crates were scattered every which way but it was dark and shadows danced across the floor and ceiling.

Jacques closed the trap door and it was invisible against the rest of the floor. He wondered how long it would it take for someone, or some*ones*, to come and collect him, let alone where would he go, and what was he supposed to do? Also, why was Harrison so upset about a secret? Clearly it was something big but he had never seen him like that. This was all very confusing, and all Jac wanted to do right now was be home with his sister and mother, grieving for his father. He had not gotten along with the man, but he still loved him. He was his father, after all.

Jac suddenly realized that all of his effects were still on the coach in front of Harrison's building and he had no idea if the driver would tip off the authorities about his little visit. Jac was a fairly good guesser about distances, so he was sure he wasn't too far from the coach and the driver. Even if he got to the driver before the news went out, how could he be sure that he could pay for the driver's silence?

"Shit." Jacques cussed to no one. He looked around for a door and managed to find one but it was locked with a keyhole on both sides. "Damn it all!" Jac slammed on the door as he shouted, his anger boiling over, but just then he heard a click and the door swung open. "Huh, that was odd..." Jac thought, but wasn't about to look a gift horse in the mouth.

He was still in the warehouse district of the capital and, if he was right, a disused area. Jac was grateful his coat was black; it would make it easier to make his way through the alleys. He slunk around the alleys and side streets, avoiding the main roads as much as possible. Jacques turned his collar up when he had to pass by people, hoping they would ignore someone who wasn't looking for trouble. Thanking the gods, Jac managed to get back to the coach and it looked like no one was bothering the driver, who looked very bored, sitting in his seat lazily smoking a pipe. Jac looked around quickly. There were some people on the street but no Imperial officials, at least.

Jac came up to the driver and explained that his services were no longer needed for the day and paid him extra to forget why he was in this district. The driver eyed him suspiciously but didn't question the money as Jacques pulled out his two bags and wandered off down the alley. He took a deep sigh of relief as he heard the coach driver start to wander off. Jac stopped to pull out his pistol and strapped the belt to his waist, making sure the weapon was loaded. He holstered the gun and moved a few things around in his bags so he was carrying only money and clothes. He wished he had a cloak with a hood or something, but it was something he would have to live without for the moment. Jac stashed the bigger bag behind a few garbage cans and started to make his way back to the other warehouse.

He tried to retrace his tracks back, but more people were buzzing around all of a sudden. Then he heard the third bell for the day: it was the end of the workday for most or start of the late shift for others, and he swore silently. He was suspicious enough with a noble's greatcoat, a backpack, and a gun. Nobles rode in coaches and didn't walk, let alone carry their own bags or weapons. Although weapons were becoming common, he still stuck out too much for someone not to wonder what he was doing in a working district carrying a weapon.

"Oi! What have we here?" Jac heard a loud voice say behind him. He turned to see a group of Jet Boarders. They had Skull Crackers symbols on their jackets. "I think the fancy lad here got a little lost, eh, boys?" The group started to chuckle as they advanced on him.

"Gentlemen, I am not having the best of days, so it would be in your best interest to move along and I'll pretend this never happened." The gang looked at one another and then burst out laughing.

"Fancy lad, if you think you can take on all of us, by all means, my lord." Sarcasm was deep and rich in the leader's voice. "But I doubt you can even take on me." He pulled a club from his back and laughed as he approached Jacques. He swung wildly at Jac, but something in his blood called out to him, and Jac ducked under the blow and drew his gun. With a roar akin to a thunderclap the gun went off, and the gang leader's head was blown clean off.

Jac didn't even remember pulling the trigger as he watched the corpse crumble to the ground. The rest of the gang involuntarily took a step back from him. He turned his head to look at them and before he knew it he was speaking.

"Anyone one else want to try and step up?" At this point the other men scattered and scrambled to get away from him. Jac put the gun away and turned to see the crowd of people beginning to form at the alley's edge. He quickly rushed through them and the crowd of people parted as he passed by with out so much as a word or a glance.

It had to have been almost an hour and about a mile away as Jac zigzagged across the alleyways. He finally stopped at an alcove between two buildings, and thoroughly emptied his stomach on the ground. He had gotten into fights before—even duels—and had injured two men but never killed anyone before. He was sick more from the shock of actually doing it than the act itself. His mind was reeling at the thought, but his blood was singing to him. He knew he could do it again without getting sick. Jac knew he had the power and grace of a skilled fighter within him.

"What is happening to me?" he asked himself, the gods, anyone, and no one all at once. He leaned back against the brick of the building and took a deep breath. He pulled the gun out and replaced the spent cartridge. The weapon felt so light in his hands, and it felt good, as if his whole life was building up to this point. Jacques stood up straight, spun the weapon on his finger, and holstered it without thinking.

"Ioney!" His mind suddenly filled with his sister. If they were looking for him, surely they were after his sister and mother, too. "Sorry, Harrison, I know you said you'd take care of them, but that's my job." He took off running; if it was after the third bell, Ioney would be near her favorite restaurant, The Red Tankard Inn. If he was lucky, he would be able to take the side streets and cut down travel time.

Of course, the closer he was to the nicer parts of the city would mean the more he could be scrutinized by more people and more guards, but it was a risk he would have to take. He skirted as many people he could without looking overly suspicious. Thankfully, time and luck were on his side as he managed to make it at the same time as Ioney. He was five feet in an alley when he spotted his sister.

Ioney looked much like their mother, with her dark, iron-red hair that currently had a black ribbon woven into her very long ponytail. Her form was slim and her face was very pretty. Jac had twisted a lot of younger men's arms for their continued annoyance of his sister—hence, one of the men Jac had injured in a duel. Jac was about to call out to her when a patrol of Imperial Regulars stopped her at the entrance to restaurant.

"Ms. Ioney Bokan?" the Sergeant asked as they approached. Ioney stopped, puzzled. Jac ducked against the wall and crept up to the scene.

"Yes? Can I help you?" she asked, annoyed that they had stopped her.

"Miss, you are under arrest." He waved at her to the other soldiers. One came up behind her and restrained her arms.

"What are the charges, and by whose authority?" Ioney was disgusted at being manhandled by the soldier.

"The charges are treason, and the authority comes from the Head Office of the Inquisitors, ma'am," the Sergeant replied as they put her in bindings.

"Get your hands off me! Do you have an idea what I can do to you?" There was explosive temper Ioney was famous for. She managed to swing kick behind her and tag the soldier in the groin. He fell like a wet sack of sticks as he held his manhood in his hands. The Sergeant backhanded her across the face. Ioney screamed and fell to the ground, and before Jac knew what he was doing, he had turned the corner and fired his pistol.

The Sergeant took the bullet to his neck and fell to his knees, grasping his wound. With the Sergeant dying, and one of their fellows crumbled into a crying ball, the other three soldiers pulled their pistols free and fired at Jac. He ducked and spun to his right and fired a second time, taking out another soldier with a hit to his chest. The two remaining only had single-shot pistols and had to stop, break open the guns, and reload. Jacques didn't have to stop, and he fired twice more with out pausing, taking out the last two soldiers combat capable. He ran over to his sister, who was still shackled, and then turned to the soldier and pulled him to his knees. The man was trying to struggle with him and Jac backhanded him with his pistol across the face and he fell back to the ground. Jac relieved him of his keys and ammo pouch; just in case.

By this time the street had cleared out after the seven bullets had ripped through the air, and Ioney had dragged herself to her knees.

"Jacques, what in the Hells are you doing?" she asked, stunned, as blood dripped from the corner of her mouth.

"I am getting us out of here, Ioney, so stay still so I can get these binders off you." Jac had to try several keys before they cuffs fell off. "Come on, I'm sure more are coming now."

"But you killed those men, Jac. How could you do that?" she asked as he helped her to her feet and they walked away after he holstered his gun.

"I didn't have a choice, Ioney, they were going to take you to gods-know-where and I don't want to think about what they might do to you there. We have to get off the streets for a while."

"What is going on?" Ioney was regaining her composer and her anger. "How could that man hit me? Why are they trying to arrest me for treason?"

"Ioney, I really don't know everything, but suffice to say right now I don't care. We need to get mother and get out of town and figure everything out." Ioney stopped and shrieked.

"MOTHER! OH, NO!" Ioney screamed, horrified.

"What? Ioney, we can't stop."

"No, no, no, no, no! Mother was summoned to the Black Spire, something about filling out papers after father died. Jac, you have to help her." Ioney began to cry and Jac brought her close.

"And I will, but right now I need us to be safe so I can do just that." He pulled her along with him. She was sobbing, but at least quietly. Jac had no idea where they were going or what he was going to do when they got there. He put his thoughts through a gauntlet, trying to think of anywhere safe to go for at least an hour's peace.

"*Jacques Bokan*," a voice on the wind whispered to him and he turned to an empty street to see a smirking Elf. He was wearing a dark vest and pants with army boots, and carried a simple cutlass and a set of pistols. The Elf's white-blonde hair was cut close to his skull and his right ear was pierced with five sliver rings, from lobe to tip. His dark orange eyes sparked with magic as he whispered to Jac. "*Follow me, your lives depend on it*." The magic faded and he spun to walk down the street. Jac pulled his sister to him and they followed the Elf. After turning the same corner they were stopped as six more people showed up. Two humans, a Dwarf, a half-Orc, a Halfling, and another Elf, plus the Elf with the rings in his ears they'd followed.

"Jacques Bokan, it is truly an honor." Rings bowed gracefully at his waist with a big flourish.

"How do you know me?" Jac asked suspiciously, eyeing each of them in turn. They were all dressed in dark clothes, with pistols and different weapons. The humans wielded long swords, the Dwarf had an axe (of course), while the half-Orc carried a maul and the Halfling carried a bo staff twice his size over his shoulders.

"Harrison de Bloom has sent us to fetch you and your family, although you have not made it easy on us, that is for sure." Rings chuckled and the group joined. "But I am to deliver you to an armored coach to make your escape. So if you'd please..." the Elf gestured behind him and Ioney spoke up.

"What of Mother?" Ioney asked, like a mouse asking a question of the cat. Jac sneered at them as well.

"How do I know this isn't some kind of trap, anyway?" he asked pointedly and Elf flashed a dazzling smile at him.

"I believe you humans have an expression about leaping and faiths being involved?" Rings stated and took a step forward. Jac drew his pistol with lighting-like quickness and drew the hammer back. "Ah, yes, Harrison prepared me for this."

"And how, pray tell, did he do that?" Jac wondered loudly and Rings smirked and said a single word, as though mountains, and empires, and the whole of the world stood on this one word.

"Stairs..." Jacques studied him closely for what seemed like a long time before putting his pistol away.

"I need you to take my sister to this coach and get her out of the city as quickly as you can," Jac stated as Ioney looked at him, puzzled.

"He said one word, Jac, one gods-damn word!" Her temper had returned and Jac held her for a moment and kissed her softly on the cheek.

"Do you trust me?" he asked her and she looked into his eyes and nodded. "Then believe me when I say that Harrison has sent these men. I need you to go with them while I free Mother." She took a breath like she was going to argue some more, but Jac cut her off. "Ioney Hillary Bokan, do as your big brother says. I want only to keep you safe." She had only heard Jac use her full name twice in her life and both times were incredibly important.

"Very well, but you had better be right behind me, or so help me not even the gods can save you from my wrath," she said as the black squad looked at one another.

"I am afraid the coach only leaves if both of you are there; your mother is a lost cause," Rings told them and Jac was about to lose his temper now.

"Listen to me, while I am still breathing, *Rings*, I will do everything I can to rescue her. Now, if it's your job to keep me safe, you are just going to have to come with me, then," Jac told him and the Elf sighed dramatically.

"Very well, but we'll need more then just the two of us, I am afraid. Bo, keep the lady Bokan safe and do not wait for us. I believe we can form a plan while springing the elder lady Bokan." The Halfling nodded his head and reached for Ioney's hand.

"Madam, your coach is this way. Please keep up," the Halfling stated respectfully and they started to walk away.

"Ah, hold on, Bo. Mr. Bokan, I am to understand that you are holding a book, a book I cannot allow to fall into the hands of the Empire," Rings told Jac and he remembered the book Harrison gave him.

"I'll give it to Ioney and no one else," Jac told him and Rings shrugged. Jacques fished the book out of his pocket put it in his backpack with his clothes and money and handed it to Ioney. She held on to it and Jac kissed her on the cheek. "I'll see ya soon." Ioney just nodded and Bo the Halfling led her away.

"Okay, Mr. Bokan, let us proceed." Rings grinned in a way that made Jac uncomfortable.

Chapter 7-

"All right, what I can gather," Rings started, "is that your mother is being held in the guard tower on this end of the Imperial Palace. In about twenty minutes they will be moving her in an armored coach to the Kettle."

"Damn it!" Jac swore out loud. The Kettle was the Empire's most secure prison: a floating island suspended over an active volcano. They had managed to get through the city to the east side of the palace and had hidden themselves in an abandoned house. Here there was a guard tower that had a few cells for prisoners and a barracks for about fifty men. There was a coach waiting in the tower hold, where cargo and prisoners were loaded and unloaded. "We should take the coach on the move; I think it'd be easier that way."

Rings nodded at him and they watched guards come and go for moment, and then an Inquisitor stepped out of the building. Rings ducked under the widow and shook his head. "That Inquisitor is a mage," he told Jac, who looked the man up and down. He looked like a regular Inquisitor from here as he pulled out a pipe and packed it with tobacco.

"Really, he looks like everyone else to me," Jac stated, before he watched the man summon a flame with his fingertip to light his pipe. "Oh, never mind."

"Indeed, this is going to be twice as dangerous now." Rings made a motion to the half-Orc and the Dwarf. They nodded in unison and went out the back of the house. "Once the coach moves, they will cause a distraction and we can assault them a fair bit up the road." Jac agreed as he unloaded the spent shells from his pistol and reloaded the clip, and made sure the other two were loaded as well. He flicked his wrist and the gun slammed closed. "You seem to be quite skilled with that pistol."

Jac looked over the pistol and nodded. "I'm not sure why. I mean, my father and uncle taught me how to shoot, fight, and fence. I thought myself far better with a sword in my hand than a pistol, but there is something about this gun."

"Perhaps you've waited your whole life to hold it? Perhaps everything you thought you knew about yourself is wrong and holding that weapon brings that to the surface?" Jac looked over at him and knew everything he was saying was right. "Does your blood call to you?" Rings looked at him, almost straight through him.

"What does that mean?" Jac asked and Rings grinned at him.

"Sadly, this is neither the time nor the place to explain, but after the events of today I will see what I can do to help you." Before Jac could question him more, one of the humans in black made a slight whistle and they peered up to the tower. The coach was on the move now. In it was the driver, two guards with rifles on the roof, and a unit of twenty more soldiers and three Inquisitors, one being the mage. "All right: we will follow till me fellows make the distraction then we will strike." They made their way out of the house and began to follow through connecting alleyways. They must have traveled a good two miles before Jac said anything.

"What is this distraction we're waiting on?" he asked Rings, who just pointed to another abandoned building. The half-Orc with the hammer was on the roof, holding a clay pot. Before anyone but Rings and his fellows knew, the half-Orc threw the pot to the street; it didn't so much as explode as fill the whole street with flames. "Okay, then," Jac pulled his pistol out as Rings snickered and pulled his weapons as well.

The first minute, shots rang out through the street as several soldiers fired almost blindly around and the squad in black fired into them from all sides. Jac had already fired two shots, taking out two of the closest soldiers before the Inquisitor mage formed a shield around them.

"Damn! Now this is currently a problem we are not equipped to deal with," Rings stated as he reloaded his pistol, and Jac was going to agree with him. The shield worked one way; nothing could go in, but they could fire out and they were doing well. The black squad was pinned down and it was simply a matter of time before more soldiers came. Jac was becoming angry. His mother was trapped and had gods-know-what done to her, and the people trying to help him free her were about to be captured or get killed themselves.

Then he felt his blood call to him.

This was his moment; now was the time to act.

Jac rose from behind his cover, aimed his pistol at the mage, and fired. The bullet ripped through the air with purpose. It was as if the hands of fate themselves fired that bullet. It connected with the mage's shield and smashed right through it like gossamer. Then the bullet ripped its way through the Inquisitor's chest and knocked him clear off his feet in the process.

Time seemed to stop for a moment as the soldiers, the fighters, and the other two Inquisitors watched the mage fall to the ground. Jac had no idea how he did that, and so didn't waste time in firing at the other Inquisitor, who took the shot to the shoulder. This seemed to snap them out of it and began firing again.

"I'll go to the coach, cover me!" Jac told Rings, who followed him and began get into melee with them. Jac shot one of the soldiers off the roof before shooting out the lock on the coach and slamming through the door.

Empty! The coach was empty! Jac felt his heart sink.

"Move, you fool!" He heard Rings shout as more soldiers came from behind them. Jac panicked and fired the last two shots before running. He bolted into an alley but didn't see any soldiers, so he kept running. Once he turned the corner a number of soldiers were there.

"We need him alive!" one shouted and Jac raised his gun and pulled the trigger, but nothing happened.

"Shit..." he whispered as the soldiers converged on him and started beating him.

Jacques sat chained to the table, his nose and mouth bleeding from the beating he'd received when they captured him. He didn't bother to test the chains, knowing they wouldn't be holding him for long. He'd most likely be executed in short order as an example to others. The small room he was held in was not much to look at. It had him, the table, two chairs, and the chains around his wrists and ankles. Clearly this was not a long-term holding cell, so he wasn't surprised when the door swung open and a smarmy-looking Inquisitor came strutting into the room.

As he sat down he removed his hat and slicked back his shiny black hair behind his head. "Jacques Bokan, The Fool's Own, this is certainly a pleasure," the Inquisitor smirked at him and Jacques smiled as blood dripped out of his mouth.

"I wish the feeling was mutual, Inquisitor—?" Jac asked sarcastically.

"Rodrigo, Jac, please call me Rodrigo. I like to be informal with these little chats. Oh, I hope you don't mind if I call you Jac. I know it's a bit sudden, what with us meeting only a moment ago, but I feel like I've known you for some time now, as I have been looking into your past and family. There are quite a few people with not-nice things to say about you."

"What can I say? It's my winning personality," Jac chuckled and the Inquisitor wore a wolfish smile.

"Well, it would seem that the treason charge would have been a bit much as of yesterday morning. But then you had to go ahead and kill several of the Empire's soldiers and two of my fellow Inquisitors. So, needless to say, the charge sticks up until we burn you alive in Hamiltin Square." Jac wore a dark expression at this point; he had witnessed quite a few deaths at Hamiltin Square. It was a monument to the forming of the Office of Inquisitors, as Maclin Hamiltin was first to take up the mantle and begin the training of others.

"Well, I hope it's an affair for the ages; I'd hate to be lit up at a party that's a dud," Jac said before he laughed loudly, and even Rodrigo chuckled with him.

"Gallows humor. Cute, Jac. I hope you are this cheery tomorrow. After all, clowns who die on that stage are already burnouts." Rodrigo stood and put his hat back on as he turned and walked out, laughing the whole way. Jac stuck up his middle finger at the door as it swung closed. It was a minute or two later when a group of five men came to collect Jac. They un-cuffed him from the table but left the binders on his wrists. They half walked, half dragged him through the tower, and stopped to pummel him a bit more as one of the guards had a brother killed in the exchange. At least they took him to the medic to get patched up and cleaned up before they tossed him in a cell.

The room contained a straw bed in one corner and a bucket in the other, and Jacques crawled over to the bed and collapsed. He was tired and in pain as he had received two beatings in two days. It was dusk outside and the last day bell rang throughout the city. He passed in and out of consciousness for a while and then was finally somewhat awake as the moon rose in the window. He struggled to his feet and peered out the bars.

The moon was full and the lights throughout the city looked like flickering faery light dancing across the night. Jacques wondered where Melda was, and the boy, Balin. He wondered that if the Inquisitors were out to arrest him and his family, would they have raided his estate in Muzrun? Or had they already? Were Melda and Balin imprisoned? Were they dead? Jac shook the dark thoughts from his head. Melda was a survivor she had probably gotten out in time. Belladonnas had their network of contacts and they happened to know more about what was going on than most.

Jac didn't have time to worry about them right now, although he hoped they were in good health at the very least not captured by the Empire. Now his thoughts were focused on tomorrow and, barring a miracle, he doubted he would be out of this cell before his execution tomorrow. So he was forced to think about his route to the square.

They would most likely take him in an armored coach with a patrol, so sometime between getting in the coach and getting out would be a good bet. Harrison was not going to abandon him to the Emperor's mercy, especially if all his plans hinged on Jac, though he still didn't understand anything about what Harrison had said. He had no time to read whatever book Harry had given him, let alone comprehend everything that had happened so far.

Why did he feel so good killing those men? Why did his blood call to him when he wielded his pistol? *Oh, shit...* Jac remembered that his gift from Graz was in Imperial hands. They had probably taken it apart by now to see how it functioned as it did. Any weapon that could break through a mage's shield with normal bullets was weapon that the Empire wanted.

He pressed his head against the cool metal of the bars and groaned at the world, though he knew no one was going to hear his pleas. Jac finally slumped back down into the straw and slept till the morning light. The first bell of the day rang over the city and Jacques rolled over to see light creeping into his cell. There was a jingle at the door as it swung open and Inquisitor Rodrigo stepped into the room.

"I would like to put on the record that I am against this in every way, shape, and form," he stated, not to Jac, but to whoever was stepping in behind him.

"Noted, Inquisitor," a soft female voice spoke as she entered. A woman of otherworldly beauty came through the door. Her skin was pale and her hair was long and auburn, much like those of the leaves in fall. She looked Jac up and down with eyes of the purest blue and wore a dress made of fine silk with gold inlaid with designs of flowers.

Jac stood and bowed promptly; after all, it was not often the Lady of Winter comes to see you. "I must apologize for my state, my Lady Winter; I have not had a chance to access my wardrobe as of late." The woman laughed slightly at him.

"I was warned of your sense of humor, Jacques, and I am surprised to find it as sharp as ever." She snapped her fingers and a young maiden brought in two stools; as one of the most powerful sorceresses of the world she could do just about anything she wished. Lady Winter turned her head to Rodrigo after her maid left.

"You are free to leave, Inquisitor. You are not inclined to expect a tip in your profession." Rodrigo's mouth became very thin as he tried to control his temper. He opened his mouth to speak but the Lady Winter held up her hand. "Think carefully of your next words, because I can very easily make them your last." Rodrigo simply bowed his head slightly, turned, and walked out of the cell.

"I cannot tell you how satisfying that was to see," Jac told her, wearing a stupid grin. She smiled at him and motioned to the stools, offering him to sit with her. "May I ask—to what do I owe the rare pleasure of this visit, my lady?"

"I am here as a favor. Your family provided me a service some years ago; generations to your kind, perhaps not as long-seeming to mine." Jac nodded as Lady Winter was one of the Lesser Gods who walked their realm. "I am bound to help in any way I can, but, sadly, I am of not much help to you right now. If you are to die today, I will help usher your spirit into the next world as I have done with others of your family, but..." She paused and looked at the door, and her voice came even softer. "But if today were to take a turn for the better I will see what I can do with aiding you in your quest."

"Quest? My lady, I simply wish to live through the day!" Jac scoffed and she smiled at him, much like a parent smiles at a child.

"Jacques, I am sure you are aware that many things are happening around you, much of which is beyond your control. The things that are within your control are few currently, but will be greater if today turns out how I wish it to." She took his hand in hers and looked deep into his eyes. "You've felt it, have you not? Your blood has been singing to you, wanting you to right wrongs, to spill the blood of the evil and corrupt?" Jac stared at her—how could she have known? "I will take that as a yes." Her eyes flared with magic and her hair fluttered with an unfelt wind. Jac felt the back of his hand grow cold; not unpleasantly so, but much like a cool drip of water on a hot day in the desert. "If, or when, you are able, come to my realm and I will help you how ever I am able." She stood and kissed him on the forehead and he once again felt Winter's kiss. "I wish you all the best, Jacques Bokan." Lady Winter turned toward the door and it swung open as she exited.

Jac was still unsure of what happened, but he did feel better about the events that were to unfold today. So when Rodrigo came into the room without any humor on his face, Jacques knew things were going to get interesting.

"Get up, it's time." Rodrigo told him flatly.

Jac smiled. "Aw, no witty banter? I was enjoying our little back-and-forth," Jac told him as he stood and a guard shackled him.

"Let us just say the Lady Winter chilled me some," Rodrigo stated with no humor and Jac snickered.

"See, was that so hard?" Jac laughed as the guard started to lead him out of the room and down the hall. Rodrigo was two steps behind him and he could feel him fume back there. Jac was in such a good mood, being led to his death by fire. Several soldiers, guards, and Inquisitors watched him as they lead him to an armored coach and practically threw him into it. Jac sat on the bench and looked directly at the two Inquisitors, who secured his shackles to the metal rings in the floor. The Inquisitors were clearly twins and didn't say a word.

"What do they call you guys? Egg and Yolk?" Jac laughed and the twins looked at each other. Before he finished the coach lurched forward and they were on their way down the road. They sat in silence, and the twins just stared at him. Jac yawned rudely and shook his head. "Sorry, didn't get much sleep in my new bed. Not quite what I am accustomed to, to be honest, but it had a sort of rustic charm. Felt like I was camping again, although I never slept on straw out in the woods. Moss isn't bad, but you have to watch out for rocks. Well, besides whatever else was in the forest that might wanted to eat you." Jac paused to look at the twins. "Really, nothing from either of you? I bet you two are the life of all the Inquisitor parties." Now they both frowned at him. "Aw, don't worry, boys, I'll be out of your hair soon enough."

Suddenly, an explosion rocked the ground, and coach shook. They could hear the horses panic as gunfire began to erupt all around. Bullets dinged off the armor plates on the coach and the two Inquisitors stood, pulling out their own pistols. One opened the hatch in the roof and began to climb out but was pulled the rest of the way. He screamed alarmingly as he was thrown, and his brother spotted a shadow run across the roof and fired his pistol, which was extremely loud in the confined space. He scrambled to the hatch and choked as Jac saw a hand grasp him around the neck.

"Keys!" a voice shouted at him. "Keys, arsehole, before I blow you into the afterlife," he repeated and waited a moment before putting a hole through the Inquisitor's chest. The body dropped back in and slumped on the bench. A fit-looking man came in next, wearing brightly colored, mismatched clothing and a mask with a laughing Goblin face on it. He was with a Jet Boarder gang called the Jesters. He had a pistol in one hand with a sword strapped to his waist. He removed the mask to show a young man with slightly pointed ears, and Jac guessed he was a half-Elf. "Huh, not what I expected, to be honest." He rubbed the stubble on his chin and looked over Jac with dark hazel eyes.

"Sorry to disappoint," Jacques told him as he held up his chains. "A little help would be appreciated."

"Oh, yeah, I just wanted to see what all the fuss was about," the gang member went on. "Whoever wants you must have paid two or three kings' ransoms for you."

"What?" Jac was surprised by the information.

"Oh, yeah, there are gangs, and mercenaries, I don't even what to know what else out there right now, all fighting over you. The word went out last night that anyone who delivered you unharmed to a drop point was going to collect a hefty reward. Plus, I know half the mercs out there have gotten some coin in advance or they would not be out there, trust me." The man put on an impish grin, and Jac felt that he did that often. "All right: follow me and don't fall behind. You're my meal ticket for the next year." The Jester put his mask back on, leapt through the hole, and helped Jac up and out.

The scene before him was chaos, to say the least. Imperial soldiers were fighting with a motley crew of different peoples. Soldiers of fortune had pinned down about twenty Imperials in an alley, and Jesters were buzzing through the air with Imperial Slicers, their flying boards letting them soar like birds in the sky as they fired pistols and slashed at each other with great swords and spears. An Imperial flew through the sky and board and rider crashed through a window and started a fire. A group of Skull Crackers was bashing a group of soldiers a little bit down the street but was being forced back.

Rings and company had managed to hold off a group of Inquisitors. The Elf smirked at Jacques and then kicked an Inquisitor in the face before slashing him across the stomach. He turned away from the battle and signaled to him. Jac leapt down and ducked as bullets hit the metal behind him. "Here you go, hero, I believe this is yours." Rings tossed him his gun and holster. Jac smiled as he wrapped the holster around his waist and then pulled the weapon out, and he felt like the world was all right now.

"Stop, in the name of the Emperor!" A new group of soldiers shouted as they entered the fray; Jac smiled at the turn of events. His first shot took out the Sergeant leading the men; he fell as the bullet pierced his helmet and his head snapped back. The next shot winged a soldier long enough for a Skull Cracker to smash his head in with his trademarked mace. Jac continued to fire into the melee, and continued to, if not kill his target, then wound them to be finished off.

"Come on, Payday, we need to get out of here. Can you fly a board?" the Jester asked as he stabbed through an Inquisitor's chest. Jacques wasn't sure. It had been years since he had been on a Jet Board.

"I can try," Jac told him as he broke open the gun and replaced the whole clip with a fresh one.

"Eh, good enough for me." The Jester whistled loudly and two more Jesters came down from a nearby rooftop carrying two more boards.

"Come on, Rings!" Jac shouted at him but he waved him off.

"I can find my own, Hero!" Rings shouted back as he fought off an Inquisitor. Jacques didn't have time to argue with him, so he hopped on the board and followed the Jester pasted the air combat going on currently. A few broke off to help cover them.

Several Slicers came up from the streets to chase them. Jac fired off a round at the group; the soldier just past the leader took the bullet and fell back to the ground. Then they engaged the group trying to run. The Jesters were already bloodied from breaking out Jac, and more fighting was going to wear them out quickly. Jacques swooped around the air; he hadn't been on a Jet Board since he was a teen, but it came back to him. He flew low and fired at a soldier trying to chase him. The bullet pierced his side and he spun out of control, slamming into another soldier and they fell together.

"Heads up!" Jac looked up and narrowly avoided a Jester, who came screaming past him, slashing at those that came near. "Catch up, Hero!" he shouted behind him and Jacques aimed the board for the hole that was made and tore after him. Jac fired behind him to make those chasing them think twice as he shot two more soldiers off their Slicers. They flew to the edge of city, and while they had been chased and had survived a war zone, Jacques felt free, finally free, for the first time in his life as he flew through the air, his heart beating a million miles a minute, sweat pouring off his skin. His skin felt like he was burning, but he was alive.

They landed in the slums, and quickly made their way into Jester-controlled territory. Jac emptied the spent shells from his gun and replaced them with fresh ones once they were on the ground.

"Hey, what's your name?" Jacques asked the gang member, who looked at him after removing his mask, half puzzled, half disconcerted.

"Now? You're going to ask my name *now*? After I pull you out of the frying pan, literally, now you are going to ask my name?" He chuckled as he shook his head in disbelief. "Quinn, everyone just calls me Quinn."

"Jacques Bokan. It is an honor to meet you." Jac held out his hand and Quinn raised an eyebrow.

"Normally nobles don't shake hands with the likes of me."

"This is not normal for me either, honestly," Jac told him as he holstered his pistol and they began walking, with Quinn leading. "Thanks for that, back there."

Quinn snorted and chuckled. "Oh, don't thank me yet. I'm still being paid a crazy amount of coin to deliver you to whoever is paying for you." They entered a disused tavern where a handful of other Jesters were sitting around. They all made to stand up when Quinn walked in and he motioned for them to sit down. "Easy, boys, this is Jac. He's with me." They all seemed to acknowledge him at the same time, and it was clear Quinn had authority here and Jac was a guest. Quinn took him up to the bar and they sat, as a portly man with a mustache came over.

"Usual, boss?" he asked as he set two rock glasses down.

"Yeah, but just one; we are killing time for a bit." The man poured out two glasses of a dark, amber-colored liquor before tending to someone else. Quinn passed him a glass and then slammed his own down. Jac sipped his, a fine Gnome brandy. He looked around the room. Jesters of all shapes, sizes, and races littered the room. They all had their masks off and were playing cards or just talking to one another.

"So, how much?" Jac asked after a few moments.

"How much what?" Quinn asked back, watching him for a minute.

"How much am I worth to someone like you?" Quinn raised an eyebrow and motioned to the bartender again. After he had a fresh glass he answered.

"A lot more then you are actually worth, I'm sure." Quinn sipped his glass this time and Jac narrowed his eyes at the half-Elf. The door burst open at this point at Rings and his black squad came in. Quinn loudly sighed and then finished his drink. "And here it comes to rub it in my face." Quinn tossed up his arms. "So just say it already and get it out of your system."

"Say what, pray tell?" Rings asked as walked up to the bar and leaned on it and signaled to the bartender, who pulled down a bottle from the top shelf. "That participating in the events of today would not only go well, but net you a profit? A profit that my work within the city provides?" Rings picked up the bottle, tipped it toward Quinn, and took a drink. "Because I did, indeed, explain that I did."

"Arse!" Quinn jumped off of his stool and Rings grinned widely as he set down the bottle. Quinn took a wide swing at Rings, who blocked it and twisted his arm behind him.

"Come on, little brother, you can do better than that," Rings told him as Quinn struggled against him.

"Damn it, I run the gang now, you smooth-talking git," Quinn stated as he struggled and then swept out Rings' leg. It did knock him off his feet, but Rings landed on his hands and leapt backward. Rings laughed loudly as Quinn came back at him with a hard left hook. Rings blocked the blow and they exchanged blows. Jac pulled his pistol and was about to fire when they finished.

"All right, that is quite enough, little brother," Rings stated, blocking the last blow.

"So you're brothers?" Jac asked as he holstered his gun.

"Sadly. I'm Garis and this is—" Garis Quinn started but Rings cut him off.

"You can continue to calling me Rings; it's appropriate," Rings stated with a smirk.

"Really? I told him my name!" Garis shouted at him, but Rings held up his hand at Garis.

"I am here to collect you." Garis snorted and walked to the bar. "Both of you, there is a meeting we have to attend."

"Why in the Hells do I have to go?" Garis asked, perturbed, and Rings shook his head.

"Would you like to get your payment for today's work? If not, I can keep it: I did quite a bit of work, too." Garis growled loudly.

"Fine. Lead the way, ass."

"Well, I'm glad that's settled," Jac joked and Rings shrugged.

Chapter 8-

Rings had led Jacques and Quinn down into the sewer system and into another secret tunnel. Jac was beginning to wonder how much of the city was known and how much was a secret. Rings came to a halt at a stone wall and when he pressed on one of the bricks, and the wall slid open. They entered a meeting room with a large round table and several chairs. Harrison was in the room, along with Lady Winter and an older man with a mustache and goatee of dark grey. He wore a military uniform with the Imperial seal on the jacket and a number of different medals.

"Harrison," Jac said happily as he got up from the table and they had a friendly hug. "I knew you wouldn't let me get burned alive."

"Well, you didn't exactly help me much on that front, Jacques. I told you I was going to take care of everything, and yet you still went off on your own."

"Sorry about that, but my family, my problem."

"My best friend, my family, my problem," Harrison shot back to him. They leered at each other for a minute but Jacques nodded his head at him. Then he turned to Lady Winter and bowed to her.

"I am happy to see you again, my Lady," Jac told her and she bowed her head at him.

"I am happy as well, Jacques. I hoped our plan would see you free once more," she told with a smile.

"Jac, this is Boris Krech, Imperial fifth legion, retired," Harrison introduced him.

The older man rose and bowed stiffly at his waist. "I knew your father when we were younger men; damn shame about his passing. He was quite the tactician, to be honest with you," Boris stated as they proceeded to sit around the table.

"Now, I believe we should come to order and continue with the business on the table at hand." Quinn took the opportunity to speak up.

"Ah, no offense to you all, but I just want my money and leave." Rings punched his brother in the shoulder and Quinn punched him back.

"Enough, you two," Harrison stated, eyeing them both. "Garis, I know why you are here, and you can be very valuable asset to our cause. I am offering you a chance to sit at this table as part of your payment. Your brother has explained what you really want from us. Join us and we will do everything in our power to accomplish that goal." Jacques remembered how much trouble he had talked them out of. Garis sneered but nodded as he sighed heavily.

"You're lucky my brother is with me on this one, or I'd tell you to stick it," he told them as he sat back in his chair.

"I'll take whatever luck I am given, any day," Harrison stated with a bit of a chuckle. "But returning to the matters on the table, we have freed Jacques and now we have to get him out of the city."

"I can take him through the sewers to the river and he can head north to Lady Winter's domain," Rings stated.

The Lady smiled at him. "Yes, I would like Jacques' assistance with something troubling my realm," she told the group.

"I am still not sure how much help I will be, my lady," Jacques replied.

"You will be more help then you know, I'm sure of it."

"Yes, but there are leagues between here and the Lady's realm, and the whole of the Empire will be looking for him," Boris replied and Jacques couldn't help but agree.

"Yes, especially after today's events, they will be like a rabid dog after me," Jac stated and Garis snorted loudly. "Well, I believe that the Inquisitor we met in the prison was responsible for my capture and I am sure he will be in trouble since I got away. I think he will scour the Empire looking for me."

"Yes, I'd have to agree: this does seem to be quite important to him," Lady Winter commented.

"Inquisitors notwithstanding, it is still quite dangerous to travel wanted by the Empire; we should send some men with him," Boris replied.

"Indeed. I'll gather up some of the mercenaries we contracted for the break-out and send them along with him. Have we received word of Ioney?" Harrison asked and Lady Winter nodded to him.

"I sent a sprite with the coach, and she informed me that they have not received any distress signal as of yet and will reach my borders three days hence. The glamour I cast on the coach will last far longer than it will take for her."

"What of my mother?" Jacques asked and the group looked at him.

"She was recovered while your escape was in progress," Harrison stated with a smile.

"I had cast a spell on a trinket and it allowed her to travel to my castle from her cell. I have my maids tending to her now," Lady Winter told him and Jac breathed a sigh of relief. "But, to my understanding, she was in poor condition when she arrived."

"How poor?" Jacques asked as his voice went dark.

"I'd rather not answer that, Jacques. You will see her soon enough and then you may comfort her," Lady Winter commented and Jac felt his anger rising.

"I know what you're thinking, Jac, and now is not the time," Harrison chimed in. "We need you out of the city and alive if you are going to do anything about it."

Jac sighed, his shoulders drooping. "I know, you're right," he agreed and Harrison nodded his head.

"I'll scramble some men together. You should leave in the morning. I'll gather up some supplies as well," Boris told him.

"Oh, make sure I have apples. I've been dying for one for almost nine months now," Jac told him and Harrison shook his head.

Jac had followed Rings and Garis to a manor house that Harrison had owned. Mercenaries were around keeping watch but blending in as just staff or guards. Rings seemed to know what he was doing, and now Jac was beginning to question just how long he had been involved with this whole thing. Ring pointed Jac to a room at the top of the stairs.

"That's the room you'll be staying in tonight. I managed to find your effects from the alley, plus whatever we could get out of your family's house before the Empire came in," Rings explained. Jacques was about to walk up the stairs when he stopped and turned around to look back.

"That reminds me—just how did you get my pistol back?" Jac asked and Rings wore a knowing smirk.

"Jac, we have friends everywhere, and some of my friends have no problem knifing a soldier or two for a few coins," he stated with a little chuckle. "We'll have food in the kitchen whenever you're ready. We need you in good shape to make the journey."

"Will you be coming?"

Rings raised an eyebrow, but then shook his head. "No. I have other business to see to, but we're heading more or less in the same direction, so perhaps we will meet on the path you now travel."

"You said you would help me understand just what I am," Jac stated pointedly, and Rings nodded.

"Indeed I did, but when I asked the Lady Winter just what you are, I am afraid I will be of no help, Jacques. The road to finding your place in our world is yours alone, but I do wish you the best and I will help whenever I can." Rings bowed his head at Jac, then turned and walked away without another word. Jac entered his temporary room. It was simple: a bed, a table with an accompanying chair, a washing stand, and a few bags. He went through the bags to find mostly his clothes and a sword, presumably for his trip north.

Jacques picked up the sword and unsheathed the long weapon. It was a good blade, and Jac swung it around for a moment, remembering all the training his father and uncle had put him through to be able to fight. Ever since Jac received his pistol from Graz, though, it felt wrong to hold this sword. He shook his head and replaced the blade before setting it down. It would have to do until he figured out what was going on. He washed and changed before heading back downstairs to the kitchen, where a portly woman was cooking stew.

"My lord," she said with a little bow as Jac sat down.

"That's quite all right; I am not a noble anymore. Jacques is fine," he told her as she placed a bowl of stew in front of him and he started to eat.

"Sorry. Been doing this so long, doesn't quite feel right without. I hope you understand."

"Of course. I've just had my whole world turned upside down in a matter of a few days. I am finding myself understanding quite a few things I never thought I would," he told her as he began to eat his meal in earnest. "So, are you a rebel, too?" Jac asked between bites. The woman looked at him sideways.

"I suppose I am. I'm Claire, by the by," Claire told him as she continued cooking. "I help feed those that Harrison brings to me. I guess he's been at this a while."

"I'm finding that out," Jac stated sarcastically and Claire snorted.

"We all keep secrets, dear, get over it," she told him with a motherly smile as she refilled his bowl.

"I know. Just a little shocking, is all."

"Well, just remember that he is helping you—is his secret that much of a problem now?" Jac shook his head at her. "See, all is well in the world." Jac laughed loudly.

"No, it is not, but maybe soon," he replied, continuing to eat.

Chapter 9-

The next morning, Jac led the group out of the city on horses. They rode through the countryside and into the northern forest. He had them loaded with supplies (and apples), knowing the trip would take several days. They had to take the lesser trails as it wasn't safe on the main paths, with the Imperial patrols. About two days after leaving the city and day traveling into the forest, the mercs and Jac made a small camp and Jac ate one of his apples. He hoped he'd see Ioney once they reached the Lady Winter's castle in the north. They had so much to talk about and with everything happening now, Jac honestly wondered if this was all a good idea. Jacques put his head back and down against his pack and was about to doze off and enter a dream, when—

SNAP!

Jac sat straight up, gun in hand, at the sound of a stick breaking in the forest. Some of the other mercs heard it as well, and many had weapons drawn. Jac stood slowly and looked around for something, anything, that would indicate intruders. He focused his eyes and saw something dart out of the darkness. Jac fired at it, and a human shape came rolling into the camp, wearing an Imperial uniform...

"Take the traitor alive, leave no one else!" A shout came out from the woods and gunfire erupted from all around. Jac fired into the dark as several soldiers came out of the foliage. He drew his sword and went it to the melee. He blocked and parried and slashed and swore as he cut down one soldier and another took their place. The mercs were fighting hard, but they were being cut down one at a time and soon they would be overwhelmed.

"Fall back!" Jac shouted. Seeming to run out of enemies for the moment, he fired into the crowd of advancing Imperial Regulars. Several of the mercenaries followed behind him but even with him firing at the soldiers who caught up they were still coming. They ran for what felt like hours and had lost the soldiers in the dark forest, but also lost their supplies and horses.

Jacques stopped with the small group of mercenaries in a clearing to catch their breath. It had been too long since Jac had to run that far; he kept in shape but he had always hated running. He was with about ten other men and most had lost their supplies as well. Jac looked up to the moon and stars and guessed they were about three miles from where they had made camp.

"Come—we should keep moving. We'll head west for a bit more, then continue north," Jac told the group.

"With what supplies? We lost just about everything in that attack. I understand that you are paying us, but that doesn't mean much when we just lost all of our coin," one of the mercs spoke up.

"I can pay you more, but there won't be anymore coin if we all die. Now we have to move; we can forage for more food tomorrow," Jac told them and started walking. The others mumbled but followed him.

It was a small miracle they had avoided more Imperials the next day and managed to rest for awhile, too. Jac had rationed the few supplies they had left, and thankfully one of the mercenaries was carrying a map.

"Okay. We should be about here, by Joan's Glen." Jac pointed on the map. "That means if we head northeast we'll hit the King's River."

"Won't there be patrolling boats up and down that river?" a merc asked and Jac agreed with him.

"Well, yes, but with fresh water and maybe some quick fishing I think it will be worth the risk. We can't go on for much longer with the limited supplies we have here." The mercenaries grumbled but nodded their heads in turn. "If we are lucky, the main group of soldiers has broken up and are looking for us in small groups, which we can possibly ambush and relieve of their supplies." This time the mercenaries agreed at the same time. "An hour or so and we move out," Jac ordered, picking up the map.

The men went to ready their equipment while Jac checked his pistol. He had removed the spent cartridges and replaced them with fresh ones. He didn't know if they were going to make it out of the forest but he had to keep going. Jac had to try and avenge his family's wrongs, but he didn't have an idea how he was going to do that. He snapped his wrist and closed the gun and happened to look up at a bird singing in the midday sun. A flutter of light passed and he swore he saw an Angel, but the Angels were allies of the Empire since the first days.

Jacques walked a little closer and definitely saw her standing high on a tree branch. She was shouting at him, but only a few were gifted enough to hear Angels. She was staring right at him, in a dress of blues and purples, her wings at full length behind as she silently shouted at him.

RUN...

Jac heard the wind whisper to him and he pulled his pistol out and turned back to see Imperial soldiers almost on top of the camp.

"RUN FOR IT!" he shouted as he fired at the soldiers. He watched as a few went running into the forest, but a few turned to fight. Jac fired one more shot before running off. Bullets crossed through the air and hit trees near him as he fled. A few mercenaries were near him, running as fast as their legs could take them. They reached a clearing and stopped as another group of soldiers waited in the clearing. Jac drew his sword as he fired his gun and charged into them.

The melee was chaotic as Jac blocked and parried while trying to slash and stab his way through them. He felled a few soldiers while his mercenaries held their own, but they were outnumbered; it was all a matter of time now. Jac was a better swordsman than the soldiers but he was growing tired, rapidly. He fired at an approaching soldier, then turned and fought one till he slashed his chest. A brief pause let him see that all but two mercenaries were down or dead and about ten more soldiers came into the fight. Jac shot, stabbed, slashed, ducked, parried, and kicked occasionally to survive.

After another minute Jacques was out of bullets in his pistol, but all but two soldiers were down and he had no more mercenaries left. He holstered his gun and gripped his sword with two hands as the soldiers came to him. Jac blocked the first blow to his right, then ducked under the one from his left and kicked the man in the stomach. The soldier doubled over as the second came around and Jac swung high; the soldier blocked with one hand and pulled a dagger with his other. Jac grabbed his wrist and pulled the soldier past him, plunging the dagger into the soldier's neck. Jacques slammed his elbow in the soldier's face and stabbed him in the chest as he fell.

Jac ripped the blade free and took a deep breath. He had no idea how he had survived the battle, but he was not about to waste the chance to get away. He sheathed his sword and switched clips in his pistol before he moved forward. Jacques was still holding his pistol when he reached the tree line and heard a gunshot. Suddenly his chest hurt and he looked down as the blood started to pool in his front. He coughed and blood came out of his mouth.

Jacques dropped to his knees as the soldier behind him, the one he had stabbed in the chest, gave his last breath and perished. Jac felt his face hit the dirt and the pain in his chest become unbearable.

His eyes slowly closed and his breathing stopped...

As Jacques slowly died, time in the forest seemed to stop. The Angel in the blue and purple dress landed softly near him, and another joined her. This Angel was a man, with glimmering sliver armor, hair of gold, and eyes gleaming red. He carried a saber alight with holy fire.

"We cannot interfere, Awen. You know that as much as I do," the male Angel told her as she crouched next to Jacques.

"I can no longer stand idly by while the world we swore to protect is destroyed from within, Bruce. This mortal can change all that," Awen told him as she brushed his hair out of his face. "Winter has gifted him with her kiss." Bruce scoffed and Awen shot him a look.

"Winter is in no better shape to change the world then we are. Besides, this one world means nothing in the grand scheme of everything," Bruce told her.

"This world is important to them, and it doesn't matter where they are in the cosmos. Every life good and pure is important, Bruce, or have you forgotten that?" Awen told him and Bruce grew angry.

"Don't you dare say I know what I have and have not forgotten! I know just what's at stake with every act we perform on this earth. This Jacques Bokan is no more good and pure as the next wealthy snob in his world."

"But he can change, Bruce. We were taught to see the light in their souls, and help them burn out the darkness."

"Do not quote our studies to me, Awen! If I had the power, I would beat down the palace doors, snuff out the evil that dwells there, and destroy the black rock until nothing but a crater was left," Bruce told her angrily. Awen stood and took his hands in hers.

"He can restore the power we so foolishly gave up."

"We swore to be allied with the Empire of Stone, not help destroy it."

"Yes, we swore, years ago. When the Empire was the embodiment of what we should for: truth, law, and order. Now it has become something unrecognizable from what it once was. This mortal has a great destiny, and we can not let him die unfulfilled." Bruce looked away from her, but she turned his gaze back to her face. "We must, my love."

Bruce's face went soft. "Awen, please, we cannot start this again."

"Please help me, Bruce, and then, perhaps, when this is all over, we can leave this world and be together again." Bruce sighed and shook his head. Awen smiled brightly at him. They walked together over to Jac and turned him on his back. Bruce put his hand on his chest and Awen put hers on his forehead. Together they focused their might into Jacques, and slowly at first, his wounds knitted closed and the internal damage was repaired. Soon Jac was alive and fit again. They stood up and Awen wrapped her arms around Bruce. "Thank you, my love." They kissed before vanishing in a flash of light.

Chapter 10-

Jac was sitting at the head of his family's dinner table. He was in his dress clothes and greatcoat and he looked at the party happening around him. His family's servants scuttled from place to place, carrying trays of food and drinks. He looked around but couldn't remember anyone's names. Jac tried to stand, but he felt a hand on his shoulder push him down.

"What are you doing, Jacques? This is your party, after all!" a familiar person told him, and he focused on his face.

"Harrison! What in the Hells is going on?" he asked his best friend.

"This is your party! You are head of the family now. We all have bow down to you." Harrison made a dramatic bow at the waist and walked backwards away from him.

"Yes, Jacques, it's a party! Have a drink, for the God's sake." He looked over at Ioney finishing a glass of wine and picking up another. She was visibly drunk. "I mean, you are the only sober person here and that needs to change, big brother," she told him as she slammed her wine.

"Ioney, what are you doing? You never drink this much!" Jac asked her and she shrugged.

"You're in charge now, what do you care about me? You got what you always wanted, so pay me no mind anymore," Ioney scoffed at him before she rose and walked away.

"Ioney! I've always cared about you!" Jacques rose from his seat to go after her but he heard a shriek behind him and turned around.

"Young man! Why are you carrying a gun? Did my idiot brother give it to you?" Jacques' mother asked angrily. Jac was puzzled then looked down to see that, indeed, he had a pistol in a holster around his waist. "You will get rid of that weapon this instant! This is no place for a firearm," she said, disgusted.

"No, this was a gift from a Dwarf, my friend...Damn it, what was his name?" Jac swore as his memory failed him.

"Swearing is unbecoming to a young man." His father placed a hand on Jac's shoulder. "A gentlemen should never swear in public and especially not in front of such beautiful ladies." Jac looked up to see a gaggle of very lovely women all swooning for him.

Great, another lecture from my father, Jac thought to himself, *and in front of a bunch of women to boot.* "Hey, wait a moment. You're dead, Father!" Jac turned toward his father, who had disappeared. Jacques spun around looking for him and saw him sitting at the head of the table with his sister, mother, and best friend.

"Of course I am dead, son. That was the only way you were ever going to sit here, but even that was too good for you. So I went ahead and destroyed the family for you. I couldn't very well leave the wealth and fortune of the Bokan family for you to squander on booze and whores, now, could I?" His father laughed his hearty laugh, and soon they all were laughing at him...

Jacques awoke in the forest, gasping for breath. He rolled over onto his stomach and curled up and coughed like he hadn't been breathing for hours. He scrambled to his feet and braced himself against a tree. Jac noticed two things right away: he was gripping his pistol so tightly his knuckles were white and it was dark now. The moon was waning in the night sky overhead, but it still shined brightly enough for him to make out shapes. Jac looked around at the battlefield before him. The mercenaries Harrison had hired lay dead, along with about two score of Imperial soldiers. Jac forced himself to release his pistol and let it drop to the ground, and he shortly followed it. His legs were weak, his body was sore, and he was very tired, very quickly. He looked at the scene before him again with a sunken expression.

"I'm sorry..." he whispered to the dead who lay before him. Jacques picked up his pistol and began walking, stumbling away from them, northward. He traveled for hours, not knowing if he was even going the correct way. Then suddenly he was out of the northern forest and in the Horse Steppes and had blundered onto the main road. He walked for a time before exhaustion finally got him and Jac tripped over a rock. He landed in the dirt and rolled onto his back and blacked out...

Rodrigo had been called back to the Imperial Palace, to a level he, admittedly, had not yet seen. He walked into a balcony courtyard where the Supreme Inquisitor was currently. She had a range set up for throwing daggers, with a target large enough for a man to be strapped to. Indeed, today there was a man strapped to her current target. Inquisitor Jasmine pulled from a whiskey bottle, then picked up three daggers and threw them at the board. The daggers hit the board by the man's neck and down this right shoulder, and Rodrigo noticed the gag in the man's mouth to stop him from screaming.

"You had better have good news, Rodrigo. This catastrophe with Jacques has put a lot of pressure on me," Jasmine told him as he bowed respectfully.

"I would like to point out my idea to have him assault his mother's caravan worked, and I pointed out that Lady Winter was there the day he escaped to have a private conversion with him."

"Oh, go blow smoke up someone else's ass, Rodrigo. Lady Winter has been an ally to the Empire before there was one. And even if we could do anything about her, Lord Summer would march into the Capital like a wildfire." She threw three more daggers, hitting near the man's left side under his armpit.

"Well, I am afraid, then, I do not have good news. I sent a battalion of hundred soldiers into the northern forest after him and only about thirty men came back. There were a number of mercenaries with him and Jacques has since disappeared. Also, all the mercenaries we could discover were all dead by the time we found them."

Jasmine growled loudly and threw six daggers, all missing the man narrowly. "Do you know why I am out here right now, Rodrigo?" He shook his head once. "Because I am so good at throwing a dagger that I can hit a man without even trying. I practice not hitting them to retain my skills." She spun and unleashed a flurry of daggers, each one barely missing the man. "You are running out of time, Rodrigo. Next time you leave this city, bring me Jacques Bokan, or don't bother coming back at all." To make her point she picked up a single dagger and flung it without bothering to look. It hit the man square in his heart. His eyes screamed with pain as he slumped over and blood pooled on the ground. "Do I make myself clear?"

"Yes, ma'am."

Chapter 11-

Jac felt like he was drifting across the ground. He dreamed of Angels and soldiers; of war and industry and his family...

He groaned with discomfort and stirred in a bed. It was dark and he tried to sit up but he felt hands on his bare chest.

"Shh, you need to rest," a soothing voice told him as she pushed him down in the bed. He felt a cup at his lips. "Here, drink this; it will help." The water was cool and Jac took a long drink. "Rest now." Jac closed his eyes again and awoke when daylight hit his face.

He tried to turn but the pain in shoulder was too intense and his eyes opened wide. His shirt was gone, his right arm was in a sling and wrapped tightly, and his entire chest was a big dark purple bruise and his face felt sore. Jac finally got a chance to look around.

His was a small room, just big enough for the bed and a corner table and chair. There was pitcher on the table with a cup next to it. A small window straight across from him told him the sun was coming up. There was a shirt on the chair but he knew it wasn't his. Jac swung his legs over the edge of the bed, and noticed his boots were underneath. His pants were a mess: they were dirty and both knees had huge rips across them, along with the scratched and cut bottoms from the underbrush from the forest.

Jac slipped his boots on carefully and managed to throw the shirt over his shoulders. He was lucky it was button-down as he slipped his left arm into the shirt sleeve. He walked out of the room into a larger living area, noticing it was a smaller cottage. There was a fireplace to the left with a kitchen next to it and a table and chairs in the center of the room with a pair of rocking chairs on the right of the room. Jacques noticed his gun was on the table center when the front door opened.

A very pretty woman came in. She had light skin with dirty blonde hair held in a modest ponytail. She wore a simple dress the color of wheat and had a chain around her neck that plunged into her dress and didn't reveal what was at the end.

"Oh, you're awake," she said with a soft voice like honey and with a smile akin to sunshine.

"Ah, yes. I am guessing I have you to thank for my aid?" Jac asked as she walked to the kitchen and set down a bundle she was holding.

"Yes. I was training to become a doctor but I could no longer afford my lessons, sadly," she replied as she opened the package. Suddenly a gruff older man came in; he was balding with gray-black hair and a thick beard with a scar across the left side of his face.

"I see you're awake! Good, I was afraid you won't wake, but Janna here instructed me otherwise."

"Oh, Father, stop. I simply put my knowledge of medicine to use," Janna scolded him playfully as her father smirked and motioned to the table. Jac sat with him.

"I'm Frank Kage, and this is my daughter, Janna." She looked back to smile at him, the kind of smile that could warm you on a cold day. "I was on my way back from the Capital Bazaar when I found you lying in the road. May I ask what happened?"

"Um, Ben. Please call me Ben," Jacques lied, even though these people had cared for him. "I was with a small caravan heading north when we were set upon by bandits." Frank raised an eyebrow at him.

"Hmm, that might explain all the soldiers running around the forest like chickens with their heads cut off. I heard a dangerous criminal had escaped from the Capital and was heading north as well."

"Perhaps he was the one who attacked us. I tried to get my fellows out of there but we got separated and I ran till I could no longer run," Jacques explained and Frank watched him carefully but nodded his head anyway.

"Well, you are welcome here on my lands till you are ready to leave. Janna will take care of you till then."

"I'm afraid I have no way to pay you back for your kindness," Jacques explained and Frank just shrugged at him.

"I'm sure you'll find a way; don't concern yourself with it currently." Frank smiled as he stood and turned to Janna and kissed her on the cheek before leaving.

She produced a bowl of a fruit and placed it on the table, and Jac spotted a shiny green apple on top. He grabbed the apple and took a bite without thinking.

He chewed the piece and swallowed before thinking about it. "Sorry, I have a weakness for apples." Janna waved it off and sat next to him.

"It's fine. You were asleep for two days, and I am a little surprised you are not hungrier, to be honest. And feel free, the farm here is very fertile—we grow lots of different fruits and grains," Janna told him as she grabbed a peach and began cutting into it. "I haven't seen any cases like yours, to be sure. You look like you were shot in the chest but it didn't leave a wound, just the bruising on your arm and chest. I thought perhaps you had fallen from a tree and broken a bone but they seem to be intact as well. I wrapped your arm up to stop you from hurting yourself further but I don't believe it needs to be on anymore."

"I am afraid I cannot tell you what exactly happened. Perhaps all of this damage came from the fall when I passed out?" Jac asked and Janna thought to herself as she ate a piece of the peach.

"Perhaps that might explain the bruising, but you should rest for a few days and I'll see what I can do for a meal for you." She smiled again, and Jac felt his heart melt a little as he smiled back. Janna stood and wandered about the kitchen for a bit as she got soup ready. Jac finished his apple and thought about his circumstances for a bit.

The last thing he remembered was, indeed, being shot in the chest, and dying on the ground, but once he had succumbed to the blood loss he woke up and it was as though nothing happened. He had only ever heard of that happening when Angels were involved. Sure, clerics could channel magic from the gods and heal the sick and wounded, even bring people back from the dead from time to time, but this was a whole different level of magic. Not only was he brought back from the dead but was healed completely, minus a few bruises he was sure he picked up from the fall before he blacked out.

Jac reached out for his pistol and pulled it from its holster. There was not a mark on it. Graz had done a fine job indeed with the magical runes. Jac emptied out the cartridges, put them in the pouch, and put the weapon away. Janna had come over with a bowl of hearty soup.

"You seem quite attached to that weapon. If I was a lesser woman I'd be a little jealous, to be honest." Jac chuckled as he pushed it out of the way for the soup.

"It was a gift from a friend," Jac stated as he began to clumsily spoon his soup.

"When my father brought you in, you were gripping it so tightly I practically had to pry your fingers off of it to take it," she told him as she took the soup and began feeding him. "This reminds me of when I had to take care of the elderly back in the Capital."

"My right hand is my strong hand," Jac explained in between bites.

"It's fine. Reminds me of better times with my husband."Jac raised an eyebrow.

Jac raised an eyebrow. "You're married?" he asked and she gave him a sad smile.

"I was. He worked in one of factories, making gears and switches so the nobles could keep their pristine lives away from the filth on the streets," Janna grumbled and Jac felt bad as he asked his question.

"May I ask what happened?" She looked surprised but sighed heavily.

"He wanted to make our lives more secure, so he got caught up with smuggling special parts to a rebel contact. The money was plenty but an Inquisitor by the name of Belt caught him, while two of his other Inquisitor buddies beat and tortured him for two days before they shot him with a firing squad. I was held in a cell for over a week after. I found out later they had burned my sweet Scott and threw his ashes in the river. My father was a soldier and came to bring me back home. I've been here for five years now," Janna explained with sadness.

"For what's it worth, I am sorry," Jac told her and she smiled brightly again.

"Well, can't live in the past. I stay here and help people in the village when they get sick or injured and just try and do as much good as I can," Janna explained as Jac finished the soup and she stood up and got herself a bowl. She sat back down and looked over at his gun. "Are you a soldier as well?" Jac chuckled and shook his head.

"No, and to be honest I don't what I am anymore." He picked up the weapon and looked at it in his hands. "My father and uncle taught me many things, but I just got swept up with this whole thing out of happenstance." Janna cocked her head to the side and looked at him, puzzled.

"What whole thing, Ben?" That took Jac off guard.

"Oh, being with the caravan and heading north. I figured I would spend my days in the Capital till the gods sought fit to call me," Jac half-lied to her.

"You had fairly fancy clothes for just a caravan guard," she puzzled to him as she blew on the hot soup.

"Got lucky in a card game, took a noble's spare set of clothes from him. Paid a pretty penny to a tailor to have them fitted for me, but made me look professional." Jac smirked; he didn't know where all these lies were coming from. Janna giggled at him, and it made his heart skip.

"Well, I am glad one of those nobles finally got what was coming to them. Selfish bastards, the whole lot of them." Janna declared and Jac smiled and nodded with her. He felt awful...

Later that day, Janna removed the sling and unwrapped his arm. It hurt to move it but Jac muscled his way through the pain. It was good that he was getting a chance to move his arm, but it was so stiff from being wrapped up for days that it was slow going, on top of the fact of the massive bruising he had over his arm and chest.

"I must thank you again. I don't know what would have happened to me if your father hadn't come along when he had," Jac told her as she rubbed a minty-smelling compound on his bruises. After a moment the pain was soothed to a dull ache and he was able to properly put on a shirt.

"It's okay. My father has taught me to be kind and gentle. Mother always said he came back from the army a changed man," she told him as she put away the minty stuff.

"What did she mean?" Jac asked, sitting back in the chair. Janna thought for a moment, then just shrugged.

"Neither of them would say, to be honest, just that he came back different. But he came back with enough coin to purchase a large plot of land and then he married my mother. We practically feed the town and help anyone passing through if they need it," Janna told him as she checked on a roasted rabbit. Jac nodded his head, knowing that a few things in one's life can turn them upside down. Dinner was quiet and Jac was tired again before he knew it. He bid Janna a good night and went back into the small room and lay down.

That night he continued to dream of Angels, Inquisitors, and Janna. Why was he dreaming of Janna? He wanted to think about Melda, but she escaped his thoughts that night. He awoke with the sun and got dressed with new clothes that Janna must have left out for him while he slept: a new shirt, pants, and boots, with a vest as well. He came out of the small room, now dressed, to Janna cooking breakfast. She smiled her warm smile at him.

"Good morning."

"Good morning," Jac said as he sat down. Janna set down a plate with some bread and cheese. "I was hoping I could get the copper tour today." Jac told her and she gave him a queer look.

"If you're feeling up to it, but I doubt there is a whole lot here to see, honestly," Janna told him as she cooked something in the fireplace. "There is just my father's estate and the village, along with the other farmers, but that happens to be about it."

"Well, I'm sure it's still a charming little place," Jac said as he started to eat. Janna chuckled.

"You've never lived in a small town, have you, Ben?" Janna asked him as she finished cooking and sat down a plate of roasted meat in front of both of them.

"No, I'm afraid not. I lived in the capital most of my life, and I was in Muzrun to the east for a couple of years. It was my father's sudden passing that brought me back to the capital." Jac explained, his head wrapping around everything again.

"Oh. I am sorry to hear about your father."

"Yeah, me too." Jac smiled sadly at her and they ate in silence for the rest of the morning. The sun crested and the morning was bright as Jac walked out of the small house. A bit away was a larger manor house that was two stories and rather wide. There was an orchard and farmland behind the houses and a pasture with some farm animals wandering around connected to a barn. "So, you live here on your own?"

"Well, yes, but my family is right next door, and the village is only about a five minute walk down the road. Would you like to come and see?" Janna asked, pointing down the road.

"Of course." Jac smiled at her but thought for a second. "Just a moment, though." She looked at him, puzzled, as he returned to the house and came back, strapping the gun around his waist. "Sorry, I've been using it so long that I don't feel quite clothed without it."

"Well, I doubt we'll find much danger in the village, but when I came back home I carried my doctor bag around with me for months," Janna said as she held out her arm and Jac put his through hers and they walked down the road. It led between the two open pastures. There were two farmhands handling the animals in the pasture and they waved as they began to walk. Janna waved back. "My brother should be coming back from his trip to the north today, and I'd like to introduce you if you'd allow me."

"Of course, I'd like to meet the rest of your family."

"It's just my mother and brother left. Do you have any family?"

"Yes: my mother and my sister. I sent them north after my father passed. I have family up that way. So I picked up guard work as well to make the trip and get paid for it, too." Jac smiled at her and she nodded as her family lands ended and they were met by the village. A few one-story houses, a tavern, general shop, town hall, and some kind of odd workshop were scattered around.

"Well, here we are! Welcome to the village of Kreet." Jac just smiled at her knowingly.

"I told you: charming." He laughed a bit with her and she couldn't help but join in with him. They walked just up the road to see the outstretch of farmland beyond the village.

"We have a coach come through about once a month and some traders and caravans come through to stock up a bit before they reach the fork for the river, or travel the rest of the rolling grasslands that head north." They walked back into town and Janna introduced Jac to some of the villagers as Ben Kaleb, which was the name of a boy Jac had gone to school with. Several people looked at his gun but didn't question him about it. Jac was genuinely happy to be here with Janna; she made him happy.

After another day of rest, most of the bruises on Jac's chest had faded and his pain had greatly subsided. Jac asked if he could help Janna, who was more than happy to boss him around. Jac learned quickly how to wash clothes and the proper way to dry them, along with learning how to sew a holes and buttons, after a lot of trail and error (and many pricked fingers later). That night they had talked more and Jacques had opened up more about his family and his friends, but still felt terrible about lying to her on a few things. While Jac had helped out around Janna's home he also helped Frank and the farmhands work the fields and orchards. He couldn't remember a time he felt so tired, but Frank and Janna were more than happy to have some help and Jac was happy to spend time with Janna.

After a few days Frank sent them both to the store for a number of things. Janna had left Jac in front of the general store while she placed an order and Jac watched a small boy play with some kind of puzzle game that looked shiny and new. Then came in seven riders: six men and one woman, riding at full speed. Jac knew they weren't going to stop in time. He ran with all the speed he could muster and picked up the boy and was out of the way with a second to spare. His temper caught the better of him and he shouted at them.

"What in the Hells do you think you are doing?" Jac bellowed at the group after set the boy down. His mother came and whisked him away quickly. The riders all seemed to be dressed in blacks or grays, and wore red sashes and long dusters. They stopped and turned to him. One of the men, with an ugly face and equally ugly scar that started at his left lip and rose to his chin, rode up to him.

"What did you say, boy?" The man was clearly older but Jac stood his ground. He suppressed his blood calling to him.

"I *said*, what do you think you're doing? You were riding to fast! You could have killed that boy!" Jac told him, staring him down.

"He shouldn't have been in the street. Fool boy would have got what's comin' to him," the man said as he spit at Jacques' feet and his hand went slowly to his gun. "You want to take his place? Hmm?" The ugly man pulled back his coat to show the pistol at his waist. Another man came riding up; he was younger and handsomer but had a dark look in his eyes that made Jac's skin crawl.

"Come, Hesh, we have business elsewhere." Hesh spit again but nodded and turned around. The younger man stayed. "You look new, Mr. ...?"

"Kaleb, Ben Kaleb." Jac continued to lie, but his blood screamed at him to reveal his true name.

"Well, Mr. Kaleb, you see, we run things around here. So I suggest you forget this little encounter, and avoid us from now on and we'll be just fine." He smiled an evil smile with perfect white teeth and Jac felt his sinister nature and a wisp of magic come off of him.

"I'll remember this, you can count on it," Jac told him as he stared the man down, who continued to smile. He tipped his wide-brim hat to him and turned back toward his group as they headed toward the tavern. The woman stayed and stared at him for a moment. She was clearly not from around here—her skin was dark caramel color and she was quite lovely, wearing tight clothes with a round-brim hat and watched him with eyes just as dark as the man's. She had two whips strapped to each hip and a pistol across her chest. She nodded her head slightly to Jac as though they had sized each other up and Jac felt compelled to nod back, as though she was a worthy foe.

Janna came rushing out to him from the store once they were gone and pulled him toward the farm. "Do you have any idea who those people are?" Janna asked, with equal parts terror and anger.

"A group of thugs, nothing more," Jac replied as he let her lead him.

"They are a group of bandits who terrorize us! We pay them off so they leave us alone," Janna explained as they reached her home. "They came about two years ago now. At first we resisted and called for a magistrate but they would come and leave just as quickly. The Empire doesn't care about us in the middle of nowhere."

"It's still wrong, Janna," Jac told her and she nodded at him.

"What were you about to do, shoot them?" Janna asked in all seriousness.

"Well, that would have been fairly impressive since my gun is empty." Jac pulled his pistol and broke it open to show her the empty clip.

"You shouted at them with an empty gun?" she yelled at him, and he smirked at her.

"They didn't know that," Jac told her and couldn't help but laugh.

"You have got to be the bravest, or most foolish, man I've met," she told him.

"I'm probably quite a bit of both," Jac said as he loaded his gun, just as Frank and woman who looked very much like Janna came walking up.

"I heard that our guests are back in town," Frank stated as he approached them and eyed Jac's gun.

"May I accompany you, sir? I'd very much like the chance to see the bandits in action."

"I believe you've seen quite enough," Janna told him.

"Introduced yourself already? Well, I can't stop a man from walking with me, that's for sure. But I do suggest that you just stay clear of them. Last thing we need in this town is a shootout," Frank told him.

"I'll be there just in case. Least I can do for hospitality," Jac replied as he closed the gun and holstered it. Frank nodded at him and turned toward Janna.

"Get your bag. I don't want anything to happen any more than you but we should be ready, just in case," he told her and she nodded sadly and went into her cottage.

"Ma'am, I am Ben, and I am very sorry we have to meet like this." Jac turned to Janna's mother and bowed to her. She was caught off-guard but tipped her head to him.

"Margret. Ben, I am happy to meet you, as well. I am grateful you wish to look after my husband," she told him and Jac smiled at her.

"If he hadn't have happened upon me I'd most likely be dead now." Janna returned with a large bag that she had slung over her shoulder. "Well, no time like the present." Jac motioned toward the little town and they walked off toward the tavern. Frank met with two other men; one was bald with a thick mustache and another, younger man wearing noble's clothes from the capital. They spoke briefly before entering. Jac waited out side across the street with Janna by the general store. The woman came out of the tavern and stared at Jac with arms folded. Jac wanted to draw his pistol and shoot but he resisted.

A group of children came running down the street, playing some kind of game, and a small girl bumped into the woman. She looked at the girl, who had fallen on her rear. The woman grabbed her up off the ground and led her to the middle of the street, tossed her down, and drew one of her whips. The small girl began crying as the woman cracked her whip before drawing it back above her head. Jac moved before he could think about it. He rushed and grabbed the end of the whip and held it taut before the woman could lash the terrified child, who got up and ran away.

Jac ripped the whip back and drew his pistol at the same time, so when the woman refused to let go and had to turn around to avoid being sent to the ground, she was met with his pistol. He pulled the hammer back slowly as they made eye contact and the woman smirked devilishly at him. The door to the tavern burst open and two of the other bandits rushed out, waving their pistols at Jac. He could tell they had been drinking and would not be the best shots.

"Let go of Inga's whip, punk," one of the bandits slurred. Jac sneered but didn't let go.

"What do you think your odds are?" he asked aloud and the two bandits dumbly looked at each other.

"Wha'?" the other one asked. Jac sighed loudly and Inga wore an expression akin to her feeling his pain.

"I have an eight-shot repeater, you have single shot pistols. What are the odds that I can take out all of you before you are able to shoot me? Because, to be completely honest with you, I think my odds are pretty good."

"You ain't got to bring your fancy math in this," the other bandit said and Jac looked at Inga.

"Why do you put up with these two?" he asked.

She shrugged. "They are loyal and do what they are told," Inga told him with a voice that was full of dark malevolence.

"You need to spring for ones with some more brains."

"Is that so...*Jac*?" Inga whispered and he was about to pull the trigger when the leader of the group came out.

"Okay, let's everybody calm the Hells down," he said as he pushed down the two pistols. "Inga, I know you caused all this so stand down already. I am not about to shoot up the town just yet." She wore an angry look but calmly stood straight and Jac let go of the whip and lowered his pistol but didn't holster it. "Now, Mr. Kaleb, I thought I made myself clear, but evidently you have a problem hearing, so now you have a choice."

Jac glanced over to him and angry look. "What choice is that?" he asked with a bit of a growl.

"Tomorrow we are going to come into town and you can die like a man with some honor, or you can run like a coward. That would be the choice I am giving you." He flashed his bright-evil smile, then whistled loudly and the rest of the bandits came out of the tavern and got on their horses. Inga was the last to leave. She blew him a kiss and winked at him before she left.

"Well. I'm sure *that* could have gone better."

Chapter 12-

Inside the tavern, Jac sat with Frank, Janna, and the two other men. The older man with the mustache was Eggbert Tomas, the owner of the general store, and the younger man was Tytis Fib; his father, Harold was the owner of the workshop and smithy in town. Tytis was responsible the business operations while his father and brother did all labor for the shop.

"Well, Edwin, their leader clearly ordered Inga out into the street to see if I would do something," Jac told him after he found out the handsome man's name. "He didn't even seem mad I had made a scene. And the two idiots he sent out couldn't hit the broad side of a barn, so I am really not clear if he wanted a firefight to happen or not."

"As fascinating as that assumption is, we have bigger problems now," Tytis sighed as he rested his head on right hand.

"Indeed. Even if you stay and fight them tomorrow, Ben, they will punish the town regardless," Eggbert declared as he took a sip of whiskey.

"Then I'll deal with them tonight. They can't be that far from town," Jac said and got looks from everyone.

"What are you going to do, son? Just charge into the camp and demand to duel them one at a time?" Eggbert asked with a bit of a chuckle.

"No, I'll ambush them in their camp, or wherever they sleep." Frank looked at him with a queer look. That's where Janna got that look, Jac suspected. "Unless you all want a gun fight in the middle of town, wherein I have to kill all of them without a plan?" There was a bit of grumbling around the table. "Okay. So we all agree, then?" Jac asked and the table quietly nodded their heads.

Jac led the way back to Janna's home after getting a few things from Eggbert's store. He had changed into darker clothing and carried a backpack with a few things he thought he would need. Janna was waiting for him when he left the small room and she did not seem pleased.

"Why do you have to go?" she asked him pointedly.

"Because if I don't, the town has to pay for me, and I'm not one to run away," he told her as he checked if the other two clips for his pistol were loaded. "Does your father have a horse I can borrow for the evening?"

"I don't want you to go," she told him softly and Jac stopped and sighed.

"I don't want to go and kill those people, Janna."

"Then why are you?" He could see tears beginning to form in her eyes.

"Because not too long ago I was not a nice person, and now I can change the things I don't like instead of standing idly by. I am going to help keep your family safe."

"But you can just leave! My father will just have to pay more for a while and soon they will forget about you." Tears began to fall from her eyes. Jac stood close to her and wiped the tears away.

"I am doing this for you, Janna. You saved me, and now it's my chance to return the favor. Please trust me when I say I want to come back from this unscathed as much as you do."

"Please..." Janna whispered to him.

He lifted up her chin. "I will be fine, promise." He smirked at her and she rose up, kissed him on the cheek, and walked quickly to her room. Jac sighed as continued to get ready. He loaded the extra clips for his gun and was about to leave when Janna came back. She held a dark green cloak with a hood.

"This was Scott's. He liked to hunt. I hope it keeps you safe." She handed it to him and Jac threw it over his shoulders. It fit like it was meant for him.

"Thank you, Janna. I know it will keep me safe." He ran his hand across her cheek. She smiled and Jac smiled back at her. They walked out and saw Frank with two horses, and he was dressed for hunting as well, with a rifle slung over his back.

"Ready, son?" Frank asked and Jac shook his head.

"No, you can't go. This is my mess, Frank, and I will clean it up," Jac told him and Frank laughed.

"This is my home, Ben. You can't tell me what I can and cannot do to protect it. Now, are you coming?" Jac shook his head but mounted the horse just the same.

"I'd like to say that I'm against this."

"Noted. Now let's get a move on."

Jac and Frank rode down the road as fast as they could till the trail ended and they turned off the path into the forest. Here the horses had to trot to avoid possibly tripping on the shallow holes in the path. Soon Frank had stopped them and tied off the horses, drawing his rifle. Jac put the hood up over his head and they snuck through the woods as quietly as they could. Jac had to shake off the memories of the death he dealt in the woods and when he was shot.

They came upon the camp from behind a small mound with a fallen tree at the top. Frank took off his ammo pouch and set near him as Jac drew his pistol. It was beginning to get dark but there was enough light to make out shapes of people in the woods. They had a fire started in the middle of the camp and Jac spotted a couple of the bandits from town.

"All right, cover me," Jac whispered as he slid down the mound and soundlessly snuck into the camp. He was trying to find Inga and Edwin first since she knew him, somehow, and Edwin was the leader. He heard someone laugh harshly and saw Hesh come out of a tent, stumble over a log, and look straight at Jac with narrowed eyes.

"What'n the—?" He never got to finish his thought as Jac fired and watched as the bullet pierced his forehead. His body fell backwards into the tent, collapsing it on top of him. The rest of the camp was on alert now, and Jac ducked down into the underbrush as bullets flew through the air at him. He heard Frank's rifle crack overhead and the accompanying shout from a wounded man as he fell. Jacques managed to roll out from under a bush and fire at another bandit, who clutched his chest as the bullet hit him.

"Damn it, get Inga!" Jac heard Edwin shout not that far from him. He dashed behind a tree as a few more shots were fired at him. He turned around the tree and saw Edwin commanding his men. Frank's rifle fired again and another bandit hit the ground and Jac fired into the crowd of them. Edwin pulled one of the other bandits up and he caught the bullet for him and then tossed him in the dirt.

Jac saw the magic flare around him and Edwin summoned a column of flame that streaked straight toward him. Jac rolled forward and out of the way before the ball of flame exploded behind him. Jacques fired blindly into the camp and replaced the clip as he hunched down behind a fallen tree trunk. He felt the hair on the back of his neck stand on end and leaped away from where he was crouched. A bolt of lighting smashed through the spot where Jacques just was. He knew he had to end this fight soon; Edwin was coming too close to hitting him with magic.

Frank had been firing into the camp and with Jac killing bandits as well. There were just three left and Edwin and Inga was nowhere to be found. So Jacques took a chance and rushed into the camp. He pulled the trigger as he ran; one bandit fell as he came at them, and then another and Jac collided with the remaining two, throwing Edwin off his feet, and Jac put a bullet in the last bandit.

"You fool! I am going to enjoy this," Edwin shouted at him while on the ground. He held up his hand and Jac felt the tremendous blast of wind, but it didn't move him. They looked at each other, puzzled. Edwin tried to do it again, but still nothing happened. Edwin then tried summoning an ice spike but Jac shot the ice forming in his hand. The exploding ice impaled itself in Edwin's hand and he screamed in pain as the ice shredded his flesh.

Jac put his foot on Edwin's chest and pointed the pistol at his face. "Edwin Volktin, for your crimes against innocent people I find you guilty," Jac spoke with words that were not his own.

"How did you know my name?" He was whimpering and grasping his ruined hand. Jac was puzzled—how did he know his name?

"I don't know, nor do I care." He fired the pistol, and Edwin and the threat to the village were no more. Jacques took a deep breath and looked up to the night sky as the soft wind swept through the forest. It felt good, no, *great*, but his celebration was short-lived as he looked back into the woods and saw a figure run the other way, away from him. Jac knew he had to chase the figure and he did.

He jumped over fallen logs, avoided trees and low-hanging branches while he chased the figure. Jacques was sure it was Inga out in the woods and his blood screamed for her death. He reached a clearing and stopped; it felt like a trap. Jac reloaded his pistol with the fresh clip before entering the clearing. It was dark now, with a sliver of the moon left in view, but Jac could see clear as day. Inga was standing in the middle of the clearing before him. Her hat was covering her eyes but Jac could still see her smirk.

"Your leader is dead, as are the rest of the bandits. Give up now and maybe they will just send you to the capital for trial and you won't have a lynch mob on your hands," Jac told her and she continued to smirk. Then she suddenly melted into the ground and Jac whipped around, looking for her.

"*So, Jacques, I feel that this is the best way to have a little chat away from the father of that delicious-looking little farmer's daughter.*" Jac heard her dark, wispy voice echo across the wind.

"I don't speak to phantoms and darkness. Come out and we'll have a civil talk before I shoot you down," Jac shouted to the open air.

"See, that is why I do not wish to engage you face-to-face, so to speak."

"Then speak your peace and be gone; and if I hear of you returning to the village I will spend my every waking moment hunting you down."

"Please. What do I care about a group of dirt farmers? Edwin was the only reason I stayed here as long as I did. He had potential until you blasted him into the afterlife. Now, once our business is done here, I will be leaving. Trust me, the petty lives of the villagers have no bearing on me."

"Then tell me whatever it is you wanted to and get on, will you?"

"Testy. I can see your lineage in you." The wind carried an evil chuckle. *"Jacques, you are on a path that will lead you to great power. I can boost you to greater power, power enough to squash your enemies underfoot and heel them forever."*

"I doubt very much that I will like the newfound power you are offering."

"Don't be a fool! Together with my mistress we can rule the Empire and expand it to greater power then the Empire has ever known. Our blood is the same."

"We are not the same! I'm not a filthy, lowlife scum."

"No, you're just high-life scum now. Wanted by your former friends and allies? The Empire doesn't give a fuck about you, Jacques. They don't know anymore. They have forgotten how powerful we truly are, but all we have to do is remind them of that and then watch them cower beneath us and our power!" When she shouted Jac swore he could feel where Inga was and fired. He heard her scream and rushed toward the sound. She lay on the ground at the edge of the trees and was grasping her shoulder as blood began to pool on the dirt beneath her. Jac pointed the gun at her head. "Are you going to kill me?" she asked, fear flooding her voice.

"No, although I should, and could without losing any amount of sleep, but I want you to spread the word for me. You go tell your masters and mistresses that, although I may be disgraced and hunted by former friends and allies, I am no ally of the evil and darkness you wish to spread. Now you take that message as far and wide as you can, till your legs fail or you die of exhaustion." Jacques eased the hammer back down from his pistol and turned and walked away.

"They won't ever stop hunting you!" Inga shouted as Jac walked away.

"Then I won't ever stop killing them!" Jac shouted back.

Chapter 13-

Frank and Jac had to walk the horses out of the forest and then ride them once they were back on the main road. It was close to the final bell by the time they got back to the farmstead. Janna rushed out with her mother once they were in front of the house. Jac reassured her they were fine and that the village no longer had a bandit problem. Frank asked the ladies if they could attend to the horses for a moment while he and Jac spoke privately. Janna looked at them both but obeyed.

Jac was puzzled, too, as they entered Janna's cottage, but was no longer puzzled once Frank started to move. With a lighting-quick motion, he had come up behind Jac, pulled the pistol from his holster, and cocked the hammer back before Jac knew what was happening. He turned around and took two steps back as Frank closed the door.

"Well, I have to admit I am quite impressed," Jac declared as he watched Frank.

"I was more than just a soldier in the army—I was a scout, scavenger, and a very good spy. And when you become a spy they teach you a few neat tricks," Frank told him as he sat down. Jac followed suit.

"That would explain how you could afford all this land," Jac stated and Frank nodded in agreement.

"So now is where I am going to ask you some questions, and if I don't like your answers or I think you are lying to me...Well, let's just say this conversion is going to get a lot more exciting." Frank said with a knowing glare.

"Fair enough," Jac replied coolly.

"Who are you, really? I knew of a Ben Kaleb from some of my friends in the army. Good kid; got shot, though, never made it home." Frank revealed the truth and Jac nodded his head with a chuckle.

"Of course, never fails," Jac stated out loud and Frank made a motion with the gun to get him back on point. "My real name is Jacques Bokan. The person who escaped the Capital was me and my family with some help from my best friend."

"Ah, I see. Now why did you come here?" Frank asked and Jac looked at him, puzzled.

"I didn't chose to come here; you found me in the middle of the road, half dead. And to be honest, I think early that day I was all dead." Now it was Frank's turn to look puzzled.

"How so?" he asked and Jac was at a loss for words as he shrugged his shoulders.

"Honestly, I don't know," Jac said after a moment. "I was with a group of mercenaries in the woods heading north to Lady Winter's lands when Imperial regulars ambushed us. I managed to get away with a handful of them but we were attacked and I was the only survivor till one of the dying soldiers managed to shoot me in the back. I was bleeding. I fell to the ground and I think I stopped breathing. Next thing I knew it was dark and my whole body hurt when I awoke."

"How can that be?" Frank asked and Jac shrugged his shoulders again.

"Your guess is as good as mine. I stumbled out of the woods and walked till I fell on the ground and you found me," Jac told him before continuing. "Do you believe me?"

"I am honestly not sure what to believe. I don't think you are lying to me, but I still don't like the answers I am getting." Jac made a small snort sound.

"Well, then upon our agreed terms, I believe you were going to shoot me, but I do believe I know two things for certain." Jac told him with a bit of a smirk.

"And what's that?" Frank asked, not impressed with him.

"Firstly, my gun is empty. I unloaded before we met back up at the camp. Secondly, it's my gun, and I doubt wholeheartedly that you or anyone one else can fire it, for that matter." Jac smiled widely at him. Frank narrowed his eyes, turned the pistol toward the open window, and pulled the trigger. Well, he *tried* to pull the trigger, but it wouldn't compress for him. He broke the gun open and saw all the cartridge spots empty.

"Well, I'll be."

"So what are you going to do now?" Jac asked as Frank handed him his pistol back and Jac put it in his holster.

"That is up to you. I know my daughter is quite taken with you; you wouldn't be wearing that cloak unless she was. So I'll give you a choice: you helped save my home so I am willing to overlook that you escaped custody of Imperial officials. So you can stay here, and I'm sure sooner or later you will get caught and carried off to an Imperial prison. Or...or you can leave tomorrow, just disappear and let my daughter live her life without the pain of seeing you dragged off in chains, or worse." Frank told him and Jac nodded as he stood up. "I hope you make the right choice for everyone." Frank turned and walked out the door and left Jacques sitting in the soft light of a lamp on the table.

Janna came back in after a few more moments; Jac had removed the cloak and left it on the table. He was reloading his gun and the spent clip he had used against the bandits. "What did my father say?" she asked timidly and Jac stopped what he was doing.

"The truth, which was rather sad and unfortunate. I have overstayed my welcome. I should be leaving in the morning," Jac said as he finished up with his pistol.

"What? Why? Is my father forcing you to leave?" Janna asked and Jac didn't really want to answer her. "Ben, please—"

"My name isn't Ben, Janna...It's Jacques Bokan. I was the one who escaped in the capital a few days ago." Jac reveled the truth to her and turned to face her. "I am a little surprised that soldiers or Inquisitors haven't already passed through here looking for me. If I stay Janna then I could get you and your family in trouble, too, and I wouldn't be able to live with myself if that happened."

"But I want you to stay. We could be happy if you stayed."

"And I know I would be very happy if I stayed, too, but I can't risk it, Janna. People who are looking for me know my face, and it would honestly just be a matter of time." Jac walked to her and placed his hand on the side of her face. "I can't risk hurting you. I'm sorry, but it has to be this way."

"I'll come with you," Janna told him and Jacques shook his head.

"I can't let you throw your life away. Janna, this is the best for everyone." He turned back to the table and opened the backpack Frank had lent him. Janna came up and handed him the cloak.

"Take it with you. I hope it keeps you safe and warm." Jac took her hand in his while grasping the cloak and he looked into her eyes and then they kissed. Jac had no idea why he wanted her so badly. He loved Melda, but he honestly didn't even know if she was still alive right now.

"Be with me tonight," Janna said and lead him to her room. After a time Jac brushed the hair from her face and kissed her cheek before leaving.

Chapter 14-

Jac left in the early morning, before the sun. A chill wind blew across the plains and Jac wrapped the cloak tighter around himself. He was still quite a walk from Brewer's Mill, but once he was there he could get with a caravan toward the north, or maybe barter for a horse and some supplies. Jac had taken some of the gold from the bandit camp and Edwin had an emerald around his neck he could feel was magical, but didn't know what it had done for him. Jacques didn't want to get his hopes up that it would buy him passage to Lady Winter's realm, but maybe it would get him closer.

It was probably after the first bell that Jac finally saw someone else on the road: a farmer with a cart full of hay. Jac talked him down from a silver piece to five coppers for a ride to Brewer's Mill, and it was after the middle day bell before they reached the mill. Well, Brewer's Mill was a generous term. The mill itself had burned down over twenty years ago, but a number of other, smaller mills had opened in its place. A small city had sprouted up around the mill to start with, and had only grown to a trade city since. Farmers from all around brought gain here to get processed and caravans stopped here to gather supplies before marching through Miller's Sorrow, a low valley that often flooded and happened to drown a good number of people. The town had the Empire build a wall, since a number of raids had been led against them. Now Brewer's Mill had a wall and complement of Imperial Regulars to protect them. Jacques needed a fast horse to get through the valley since it would be the rainy season soon, and then winter would come and freeze much of the land. Jac wanted many things, and to not be traveling the land through the harsh winter was one of them.

Jac walked through the bazaar, looking for merchants who were hiring for a caravan, but no such luck. A few had caravans moving out within days, but no one was looking for more hires. Jac could pay his way but caravans tended to be expensive and he didn't have much in the way of money. Next he tried to find a mage or wizard who could look at the emerald necklace, but once again no such luck. The local wizard's guild had been disbanded due to lack of membership, and no mages were bartering or running stalls in the local market.

"Shit," Jac said aloud after his fourth attempt at finding a mage. It seemed Jac was just out of luck and time, and he thought he'd seen the same couple follow him for last three shops now. They were wearing plain clothes, but had swords and pistols, so his best hope was that they were bounty hunters looking for him. The worst case was they were Inquisitors. Jac ducked into a tavern off the main road and sat in the corner of the bar. It was lit in here but not so much that Jac would be easily spotted. A few people sat at tables and a couple of people were at the bar talking with a portly Halfling who was slinging drinks.

A fair Elf maiden came up to him. "What can I get ya, love?" she asked as she quickly wiped down the table with a rag.

"I have a gold coin if you ignore me for a time," Jac told her, holding up the coin with his index and middle fingers. She looked around nervously but nodded and took his coin. Jac had a straight view of the kitchen, where a Halfling woman was cooking, and the back door. He was pretty sure he could make a run for it, if it came to that. A half-Elf male came walking into the tavern, wearing a black duster with boots and dark brown pants with an embroidered symbol of Barrin, the god of Combat and Warriors. He walked to the bar and ordered a drink, and as he lifted his coat a morning star was swinging freely from his belt. He also had a chainmail shirt on with tightly woven rings. It might be able to stop a bullet, but Jacques wasn't sure. Plus, if he was a true cleric he had magic behind him as well.

Jacques did not like how things were shaping up. He felt like bolting now and taking his chances in the town. An Elven woman came into the tavern next; she had a short sword on her back, a pistol on each hip, and dagger in her boot. She sat next to the man who just came in and began, in great detail, to go over the events of her day.

"So I woke this mornin', thinkin' to meself that we should be doin' somethin' that get s' paid. So I ate me breakfast of a poached egg and grabbed me gear here and came lookin' for ye. And where ye be at, of all places? A tavern! This not like ye. What's ta' deal here?" she asked him, and he either couldn't hear her or didn't want to.

Abruptly both doors to the tavern opened, and four figures in black great-coats and long traveler's hats entered. "Jacques Bokan, you are wanted by the Empire. Stand down and no harm will come to you." Jac smoothly placed his hand on his pistol. There were three of these goons in front of him and one at the back door.

"Something tells me that even if I say, 'I'll come quietly,' I'll still be harmed." The tavern emptied and the owner and his wife ducked behind the bar. The two half-Elves at the bar stayed, though. He drew the gun the quietly and kept it under the table.

"So you refuse?" the goon asked and Jac chuckled.

"To say the least." Jac flipped the table up and fired his pistol at the first thug. The bullet hit his head and shot his hat clean off. "Oof! You have got to kidding me." The goons were clockwork men; the one Jac had shot had his head thrown back, and it shot forward with a wicked grin. The four puppets pulled twin sabers and charged, and Jac fired another shot at the first puppet. Then the half-Elf man, in one fluid motion, drew his morning star and smashed into the abdomen of the puppet closet to him, while the woman drew both her pistols and fired two bolts of acid into the third one. The first one was damaged but still coming, and Jac kicked the chair up in front of him and the puppet slammed both of its sabers into the seat and got them stuck. Jack put his foot on the chair so it wouldn't move. It looked up at him with rubies for eyes and Jacques placed the barrel of his gun against its head. "Pray I don't find you," Jac told the machine, with the voice that wasn't his own like in the clearing, then fired the remaining six bullets into its head.

The man was finishing smashing his to pieces as the woman was pulling her short sword out of the last puppet's head. She turned to Jac and smiled a goofy smile at him, like they were playing a game. "Oi, Hero, we need to 'e gettin' before more of these mook puppet bastards come for ye," she yelled as he reloaded his pistol.

"And who the Hells are you?" Jac asked as he closed the gun. He was about to draw on them and would have if they hadn't just fought three clockwork men for him.

"Stairs," the man said in a dark voice that resonated with wisdom. Jac nodded his head and pointed to the back door. They rushed out the back as soldiers came in through the front, with the woman leading the way. Out in the street a number of soldiers were there, with a man in robes that had a hood covering his face, and Inquisitor Rodrigo.

"Hold on, I have someone to kill," Jac said as he aimed his pistol, but the other man put his hand on the pistol.

"Later," he said and Jac gritted his teeth but lowered his gun. They ran the other way across the town, till a few clockwork men began jumping on the roofs. One saw them and made a sound like a metal ping and more started to follow them.

"I'd really like to know what sort of plan you have!" Jac shouted after them.

"Oi, we need to get us to ta' ship!" the woman called out behind her.

"What ship?" Jac asked then as they rounded the corner to the main street that lead to the town's gate, an airship appeared out of nowhere. It was a massive ship connected to an equally massive air balloon. Fire spouted out from two engines that jutted out the rear, and a wing on each side keep her trim. "Never mind," Jac turned and fired at the clockwork men following them. They continued to run to the ship and saw them drop a rope ladder. They reached the rope and the woman jumped up a good distance on the rope, then Jac, and finally the other man grabbed hold.

"Hold on to your socks!" They heard someone shout over head as the ship lurched away from the city and began moving. They climbed the rope ladder as soldiers on the ground fired at them, and the crew of the ship fired back. Both parties exchanged three volleys before Jac and other two were safely on the deck.

"All right! Hit it, Avey!" a gruff older Elf shouted to a mage on the deck. He summed a bout of lighting and thrust it into some kind of generator. "Hold on, we're warping!" Jac was about to ask what he was taking about, but then the ship shuttered and Jac was knocked off his feet. His stomach felt like it was going to turn inside out and his brain felt as if it were five times too big for his head, and the pain was everywhere. It felt like it was going to last forever, when suddenly it stopped.

Jacques sucked in air like he hadn't in forever and promptly coughed loudly. "Let's not do that again!" he shouted as he writhed on deck from the ache in his bones. The crew around him laughed and went on about their business. The captain helped him up to his feet while he guffawed loudly.

"Aye, got your cherry popped, I see." The captain patted him on back forcefully, and Jac felt like he was going to vomit. "The first time is always rough if you're not used to teleporting, lad." he told Jac, who was still trying to recover his breath. "I'm Captain Jacob Craver, and this is my ship, the *Hell-born Corsair*." Jacob smiled widely at him, and Jac thought for a moment and remembered the ship was one of the most famous villains of the Empire.

"I'm on the *Corsair*?" Jac asked in a little disbelief.

"The one and the same, me boy. Now come here; sit a spell till you regain your legs." The captain led him to a bench and Jacques sat and took several deep breaths. "Best go get Reggie and Garis from below, and we can all get on with this little rebellion we got started."

Jac looked up at the captain. "Garis is here?" he asked the captain, who smiled.

"Yes. It's practically a family reunion around my ship these days," Captain Jacob stated as he pulled out a pipe and began packing it with tobacco.

"You're related to Garis? Are you his father?" When Jac asked this Jacob burst into laughter.

"I'd never spawn a child so full of malice as Garis, and Reggie is worse at times. No, lad, we're all brothers and sister. And I see you've met Iveta and Desmond," Jacob told him, pointing the half-Elves in turn.

"Yes, although I didn't know they were related or that all of you are," Jac stated. He finally felt like he was getting better. Jacob lit a match and puffed on his pipe for a moment as Garis and Rings come up from the decks below.

"Damn, Iveta, I owe you ten gold," Garis said as they reached Jac.

"Oi, pay up, sucker!" she laughed and Garis reached into a pouch.

"You bet on my life?" Jacques asked, insulted, and Garis shrugged.

"To be fair, I bet on us finding you first, but then these two said they had a good lead on you," he told him as he paid his sister the coin.

"Truly, Jacques, where have you been?" Rings/Reggie asked with a raised eyebrow.

"I was injured and some people cared for me," Jac told him as he stood, finally feeling better.

"Oi, but why were ye gone for days?" Iveta asked, pocketing her money.

"You don't know me at all but questions about my time away will be met with force, understand?" Jac shot them a menacing look and they all quietly acknowledged him.

"Well, come on, you freeloaders! Let's get this boat northward," Jacob said as he returned to the helm.

"Come, Jacques. We will bring you up to speed, so to speak," Reggie stated as he led the way.

Rodrigo walked into the ruins of the tavern. Four smashed clockwork men lay in heaps on the floor. He pinched the bridge of his nose with his forefinger and thumb and sighed. Jacques Bokan had gotten away from him, again. "I should have just shot the bastard in his cell and been done with it," he said aloud to himself. Rook, the puppeteer who controlled the clockwork men, came into the bar. Rodrigo was always uncomfortable around puppeteers, as their magical skills with the machines was almost unstudied; and Rook in particular, as he always wore robes and never showed his face.

"Inquisitor, I did not know he had allies with him. To be honest, I believed him to be alone in the town," Rook told him and Rodrigo shook his head.

"Clearly we were mistaken, as he had two competent allies and the *Corsair* on his side. Things are looking to be more involved than I had first thought," Rodrigo replied as he walked behind the bar and grabbed a bottle of whiskey and a glass. He poured the liquor, took the drink quickly, and then poured himself another. "We should head north and try to catch them before they cross into Winter's domain," Rodrigo told Rook as he sipped his drink.

"Will Lady Winter allow us into her realm?" Rook asked and Rodrigo chuckled.

"Since I believe Lady Winter to have a hand in his escape, I would have to say *no*, puppet master. Besides, with the ramifications from Lord Summer, we'd be the ones burning alive at Hamilton Square instead," Rodrigo told with a bit of a huff.

"Does Lord Summer still love Lady Winter? It has been a very long time since they have been reported to be seen with each other. Perhaps we are putting more stock in a long-dead romance then we are lead to believe." Rodrigo looked at him with a bit of a smirk; most don't speak like that of their betters very often.

"I am going to tell you something, Rook, that you can never repeat to anyone." Rodrigo found another glass and poured two more drinks. "Once, about three hundred years ago, give or take a little, honestly, an Inquisitor captured one of Winter's maidens, as she had killed a rowdy soldier. She froze his heart into a solid block of ice. Lady Winter demanded her maiden be let free and the Inquisitor refused and threatened to put Lady Winter in the cell with her maiden. Lord Summer was summoned, and dragged the Inquisitor into the open courtyard overlooking the front of the Imperial palace. He gave him a choice: let the maiden go and appease his wife with an apology or learn to fly. Well, as you know, Inquisitors are a stubborn lot and he demanded his own release, so Summer threw him off the ledge and on to the street. Inquisitors are told his story so we remember to take account of all the parties involved with arresting someone."

"Wow, I don't believe I have ever heard that one. Not even a rumor," Rook whistled as he took his drink.

"Well, we squished that story long ago. We need Winter and Summer as allies. We can't help the stories of Summer's temper but we can keep a few things for ourselves."

"So what will we do if Jacques reaches Winter's lands?" Rook asked and Rodrigo looked away.

"I am not sure, so we had better not let that happen."

Chapter 15-

Jacques had been lead to a mess hall with the Elven brothers and sister. A bowl of hot porridge was placed in front of him by a pretty cook. She winked at him before walking away and Garis eyed him.

"How do you do that?" Garis asked, pouting a little.

"She doesn't know if he's an arsehole or not, but we all know you are," Desmond told him and the group, minus Garis (clearly), laughed loudly.

"You seem to be very wise for your age, Desmond," Jacques stated, to which Desmond just shrugged faintly.

"Oi yea, 'e's just a wise ol' oak compared to the 'est of us mooks," Iveta stated, to which Desmond frowned at her and she just smiled.

"I may be a sapling to your oak when it comes to words, that is true. I just do not believe it necessary to speak of everything that comes to mind, or what happened to me, or what I've experienced throughout the day. In great, mind-numbing detail," Desmond responded and Iveta was about to draw her short sword when Jacob slapped her on the head.

"Knock it off, Ivy, there will be no fighting on my ship," Jacob told them all, eyeing each of them in turn.

"I see you're the oldest?" Jac asked as he began eating the porridge, to which Jacob nodded.

"Aye, I am," Jacob confirmed and Reggie shook his head.

"Not that he will ever let anyone of us live it down, trust me." Jac smiled and chuckled at him and Jacob sneered.

"So how are all of you related? You all look like you are from different parts of the world," Jac asked the group and they all smiled at one another.

"Well, dear ol' dad was a traveling wizard," Garis began and Reggie picked up.

90

"Yes, he traveled the world and was very handsome, so clearly you can imagine that caught the eye of many a fair maiden," Iveta picked up from here.

"Oi, can ye believe our father 'twas a pervert too; bed 'em all, to say the leas'."

"And so here we all are: Clan Leafwind," Desmond told him with raised hands.

"Yes. Of course, my mother found out about his ways when Reggie came to find us. So on his deathbed, being moments after she stabbed him a few times, she found out that he had a lot of children. Well, I wanted to meet my brothers and sisters so Reggie and myself grabbed his airship and we traveled looking for our kin," Jacob explained as he puffed on his pipe.

"But, honestly, to the matter at hand." Reggie regained control of the conversion. "We need to reach Lady Winter's realm as quickly as we can bring the speed to."

"I got this old girl at full sail, and we shouldn't jump again so soon after we did two in a row. It's too much strain on the engine. I don't want 'er to get critical or anything. If the winds are good it should be about ten days."

"Ten days?" Jac shouted. He didn't think he could wait that long.

"Sorry, lad, this ship is fast. We should be good with just about anything other then another airship chasing us. But I can't risk breaking my baby trying to get more speed out of 'er," Jacob told him, throwing up his hands.

"Very well. I can't complain; it should take less time flying than on horse or coach, anyway," Jac sighed and Garis patted him on the back.

"Don't worry. I'm sure there's something around here to keep you occupied for time."

In the Black Stone Spire, in the throne room to the Emperor, Supreme Inquisitor Jasmine was summoned. She had rarely been summoned to the throne room, and generally only spoke with Minister Partia. The Minister gave the orders the Emperor had issued, but there were far too many guards for just the Minister to be in the throne room. She was escorted through the long hall. She always admired the different banners of defeated enemies that the Empire had conquered; her favorite was of the Black Blades, a group of warrior mages she had found out and crushed.

Jasmine did not have time to admire the many banners, though, as Minister Partia was speaking with the Emperor. Once she was about ten feet away from the throne, she threw herself to her knees and held her arms out wide and her head down. "My Lord Emperor, I am honored and humbled to be in your presence."

The Emperor stood tall after she said this; his skin was gaunt and he was rail thin, and his eyes shone with a cold, dead light. The Crown of Ages sat on his head, the gold band with the Eye of Stragos positioned in the middle of the setting. It swiveled and looked at her as it sat on the ancient Elf's head. He placed his hand on her shoulder.

"Arise, child, please. I have called you because I need your bluntness." His voice was harsh and the words were spoken as though he had no air in his lungs. "If I wanted to be flattered like a whore I'd find one like Partia here." He laughed harshly with an almost wheezing cough. The Minister was a tall human with a balding head and muttonchops, and he wore the uniform of his position in the Imperial Army as head General.

"My lord, if my presence is offensive at the current time, I can be relieved," he said with a bit of a hard tone. The Emperor laughed again.

"Partia, you have always taken things too seriously. You need to find a whore yourself and get in her pants; maybe then you'd lighten up some," the Emperor told him as Jasmine stood up from the floor. She couldn't help but smile as the Emperor turned and began walking. "Please, Jasmine, follow us. I require your advice in this matter and I am afraid time is a thing we do not have at the moment." They walked around the throne and out the back of the room to a large sitting room. A massive table with a map of the Empire lay upon it with a different models and figures. A set of large, high-backed chairs were set up near a fire place with a smaller table that had a crystal bar set upon it. "Drink, Jasmine?" the Emperor asked as he poured himself some kind of red liquor.

"Whiskey. Straight, please, Your Highness." The Emperor poured her the drink and handed something to Partia as well.

"Please, Jasmine, when it is just us regard me as Thelus. It has been far too long since someone used my real name." She took the drink and nodded at him with a silly smile on her face. "I started the Empire of Stone with the understanding that I would be protecting those who couldn't protect themselves." Thelus sighed greatly, and Jasmine was sure it was the first real breath he had taken since she arrived. "I regard all creatures within my borders as my children, but as we all know there are rebellious children with the intent to knock me off my place at the head of this large family."

"And I have sworn to stop those who would try, my lord—ah, *Thelus*," Jasmine stated as she caught herself. The Emperor wore an odd smile.

"Yes, you have, Jasmine. You found enemies where I had never thought to look, honestly." He pointed to the map and the figures. "The map and figures were a gift from Lady Fall on the first anniversary of the forming of the Empire. I named it Stone in hopes that it would last as long as the Dwarves who crafted the Spire here. Several Dwarf lords swore fealty to me on this very spot. Angels sent by the gods bowed before me, and the Lords and Ladies of the Seasons swore to help me whenever they could. I united a land beset on all sides by chaos and war." Thelus sighed again, and rested his hand on Partia's shoulder and he nodded at him.

"Now I see that the Son of Bokan has fled your man again," Thelus said as he stepped up to the table and pointed to a figure wielding a sword and pistol and wearing a cloak. "He has secured fast travel and is moving to Winter's realm." Jasmine watched as the figured inched its way north across the map. "And your man Rodrigo is here." Thelus pointed to an Inquisitor figure trailing behind him. "What do you propose we do to remedy this infection, Jasmine?"

Jasmine sipped her whiskey and then took a breath. "Well, it seems that Jacques is currently moving faster then we can catch him. I am guessing he is on an airship; that's the only way he can cross Miller's Sorrow with out being caught by my man. He would need to be flying, and be flying faster then Jacques to reach him before he entered Winter's realm." Jasmine and Thelus smiled and nodded at her.

"I want to show you something." The Emperor handed Partia his drink and picked up a scroll sitting on one of the chairs. He showed it to Jasmine, who looked puzzled and excited at the same time.

"I think these will do nicely," Jasmine replied with a devilish smile.

Chapter 16-

It had been three days since the getaway from Brewer's Mill and Jac had been helping around on the ship. He got to know some of the sailors well and they had been teaching him things. Jacques had learned how to tie several knots, along with some different fighting techniques on an unstable platform, as the ship tended to lurch from time to time. Jac and Garis had been helping with different ropes that needed to be loosened and others tightened as the ship soared through the air. Braid, in the crow's nest above the deck but below the balloon, shouted down to Jacob, who was at the helm.

"Hey, Cap'ain, got contacts coming up on the port side!" he shouted down and Jac ran with Garis over to the side to look at what was coming. Jac had never seen anything like it.

It was a small boat, maybe a bit bigger then a rowboat, and it was held aloft by some kind of propeller and had a single engine that sped it on its way. There was a three-man crew as there was also a crankgun mounted to the front. The multiple-barreled gun was connected to large box of belt-fed ammo. One man could turn the crank and fire the weapon in quick succession. There were several of these little ships coming at them.

"Battle stations!" Garis shouted as he ran over to a bell and rang it loudly.

"What's coming?" Jacob shouted at them as Jac ran to where the weapons were.

"Not sure, but it's some kind of attack-boat-airship thing!" Jac shouted back at him as he grabbed a repeating rifle from their stock. Jacob had proudly boasted that they had stolen a shipment of weapons from the army a few months ago.

"You know how to fire that weapon?" Avey, the mage, asked as he grabbed his arcane pistols.

Jac snorted at him. "I ran the factory that produced these weapons. Just try and keep up." Jac shouted after him as he grabbed a loose rope from the balloon and swung up to the command deck. Avey was right behind him. The human mage had a mop of sandy blonde hair and wore a stained shirt and trousers, which seemed to be the standard uniform of the *Corsair*. Jac looked down the sight of the gun carefully at the approaching enemies. "They're too far away to be accurate while we are on this moving tub."

"HEY! THE *CORSAIR* IS NOT A TUB!" They heard Jacob shout at them and Jac chuckled to himself. "I heard that, and next time you can walk!"

"Too far for *you*, maybe," Avey said as he closed his eyes and focused his magic. His eyes shot open and he fired one of his pistols into the air with a crackle of lighting. It arced overhead and roamed the skies, gathered speed and strength, and then smashed through the lead attack ship. The lighting bolt cut right through the ship and ignited the fuel that powered the engine, exploding it in a shower of flaming debris.

"Showoff," Jac said as a ship came in range and he fired the rifle three times. Bullets hit the deck railing twice and the gunner once. The spare man came up to the gun and began firing at them. Bullets hit the ship and railing they were near, and the crew ducked and fell prone.

"No one shoots my baby and lives!" Jacob shouted as he spun the wheel to the left and slammed the port-side wing into the ship. It turned and slammed into the next ship, the propellers chopping into one another, destroying both. The ships fell to the ground and exploded on impact. "Dangerous little bastards, aren't they?"

Jac would have shouted something when the crow's nest shouted down to them, "Starboard side, new contacts!" Jac turned to see what he could only think of as a flying barge. It was large flat ship, with four propellers and two engines on each side keeping it aloft. It was full to the brim with boarders.

"Chop 'em down, lads!" Jacob shouted from the wheel as part of the crew pulled their swords and fired pistols or rifles into the horde. The first line was shot down but a second wave came roaring at them. Jac rose from the deck as a soldier came charging up the stairs; he flipped the rifle around and smashed the butt across the soldier's face. He flew over the side and plummeted to the ground, and Jac dropped the rifle and pulled out his pistol. He blocked a soldier swinging a sword at him, and put both hands on the gun and fired into the soldier. Jacques swung around, taking the sword out of his hand and knocking him down on the deck.

Reggie and Garis were helping fend off the boarders while Avey and Iveta, who was also a mage, were keeping the smaller ships at bay. Jacques joined in the melee and cut down two soldiers before one with sergeant markings confronted him. Jac blocked and parried the first two attacks and rolled under the next one. This soldier was better than the others he had fought and Jac holding his own, but all it would take would be a free soldier to stab or shoot him in the back and it would be all over. Luckily it was the sergeant who had that problem as Desmond smashed his head in with his morning star.

"Thanks," Jac told him as they turned back to back. Desmond blocked an attack with his buckler.

"You looked as though you needed some assistance," Desmond replied, swinging his mace again.

"Now if I had known this many were going to try and kill me after I became a rebel I would have done it years ago. The number of people who hate me has gone down sharply," Jac laughed as he fought.

"Humor at a time like this," Desmond snickered as he whipped his morning star from side to side, bashing soldiers every which way. Suddenly another flying barge came up from the starboard side. This one had a group of riflemen and Inquisitor Rodrigo riding through the sky. "I believe this boat is for you." Desmond turned Jac around to see the new ship and he smiled as he fired his pistol and shot one of the riflemen off the boat.

"Tell your older brother I'll be back aboard in a moment. I have to kill someone." Jacques fought his way to the rope section. He wrapped it around his foot and held it with his pistol hand and cut the rope. He was sent flying into the air, and let go of the rope and swung upside down, firing to the group of riflemen and picking off several of them before he cut the rope and landed on the deck. "Well, I'm really glad that worked," Jac said under his breath. He had no idea where this combat prowess was coming from. He charged the remaining riflemen, cutting them down in short order.

Rodrigo was the only one left. He stood with his arms crossed behind his back. "Jacques Bokan, you are under arrest in the name of the Empire of Stone and the Emperor himself. Throw down your weapons and come peacefully," he said with utmost confidence and Jacques stopped to look at him.

"You're joking, right?" Jac asked at he planted the sword into the deck and changed the clip out in his pistol. Jac flicked his wrist and the gun snapped closed and Jac pulled the blade up from the deck.

"I am afraid this is no joke, Mr. Bokan. Please throw down your weapons and I will see to it that you are justly executed as to the laws and oaths you swore to the Empire," Rodrigo told him without moving.

"Then you are a fool if you think I'm just going to lie down and die for the Empire. After what you've put my family through, you're lucky I didn't put a bullet in you back in Brewer's Mill," Jacques stated as he picked up the sword again.

"I am sure you will find that difficult, Jacques." Jac curled his upper lip and fired a snap shot at Rodrigo. The bullet hit nothing but air, as Rodrigo had disappeared. Jac whipped around, looking for him, and his fist connected with Jac's face and he stumbled a few steps away and turned to aim at him but he was gone again. Then Jacques got a swift kick to stomach, knocking him over on his back. Jac took a moment to catch his breath then had to swing his sword and connect with Rodrigo's rune blade as he appeared above him and swung down.

"You have become quite a problem, Jacques, a problem I will enjoy destroying, immensely." Jac struggled against the Inquisitor. "You and your filthy blooded kind should have been wiped out long ago. Allow me to remedy that." Rodrigo pushed harder down and the rune blade nicked Jac's left arm, drawing blood.

Jacques heard the call, then, the call his blood screamed at him—the call to right the wrongs, and obliterate evil, to destroy Rodrigo.

With strength no longer his own, Jac pushed Rodrigo off him and threw him back. Rodrigo was thrown off the edge but Jac knew he would just blink back aboard the ship. He saw where the Inquisitor was going to form again and Jac shot to his feet and pushed with his strength. Sliding across the ship like it was ice, Rodrigo formed just as Jac predicted and barely blocked the blow, which still gashed his arm. Rodrigo blinked again and Jac raised his pistol and fired at the spot. The bullet struck Rodrigo's shoulder, causing him to fall to his knees.

The Inquisitor looked up and blinked away as Jac leap at him and swung downward, smashing the wood as the landed. Jac turned and blocked Rodrigo's attack; he blinked away and Jac blocked the blow again, even more easily this time. Rodrigo swung at his head and Jac ducked under the blow and threw his shoulder into him, knocking him back.

Rodrigo sneered at him and growled. "How are you doing this?"

Jac paused, unsure himself. "I'm not sure, but I know I need to end you, and all those like you," Jac told him, then swung his blade. Rodrigo blocked and they fought for a moment. "I need to destroy your evil," Jac told him as they swung to a clash of swords.

"I am protecting my country and Emperor," Rodrigo told him and Jac snickered.

"That's why I need to kill you." Jacques knocked the runeblade away and stabbed him in the stomach. Rodrigo dropped his sword and gripped Jac's blade, but Jacques ripped it free and stepped past Rodrigo and slashed his back as he fell. He stood on the deck of the flying barge and breathed a deep sigh of relief, as though a great weight had been lifted off his shoulders, much like when he had killed Edwin. Rodrigo moaned at his feet and Jac turned him on his back.

"You will die...Jacques, and the Empire will live..." He gave his last words and last breath and died right there. Jac bowed his head slightly to his defeated foe.

"We shall see," Jac spoke to his corpse. He looked around as he tossed the sword away, reloaded his pistol, and saw that they had floated above the *Corsair*, which was still repealing boarders and fighting the smaller ships chasing it. Jac found the controls, which were fairly simple. He maneuvered the barge to float past the *Corsair*'s rear command deck and fly in front of the smaller ships. He moved the ship a bit higher in the air and then ripped out the fuel line to the front right engine and the propeller started to slow. Jac did the same to the other front engine, and oil spilled across the deck. Jac ran to the edge and jumped, while firing his pistol behind him. The bullet hit the engine and sparked, igniting the oil.

Jac grabbed ahold of one of the many ropes coming from the *Corsair* and swung to the deck as the ship above exploded and dropped into the swarm of smaller attack ships, destroying several of them as they either were crushed by the larger ship or ignited themselves by the flaming debris. Jac helped the sailors finish up the remaining soldiers, but to their credit the soldiers neither gave up nor surrendered.

Captain Jacob had his pilot come to the helm as he looked over his ship. None of his people or his family had been killed. A few were injured, including Iveta, who had caught a stray bullet to her left arm, but it was a through-and-through. Desmond had used some of his cleric magic to heal some of the most injured but his magic ran out and he grew tired after a bit, so he helped bandage wounds and lift spirits.

"Son," the good captain said as he walked up to Jacques. "That has got to be the stupidest thing I have ever seen anyone ever do."

Jac smirked and chuckled out loud. "It worked, didn't it?"

Jacob only laughed and patted him on the shoulder. "So it did, lad, so it did indeed."

Jasmine could still not believe the Emperor had spoken to her directly, let alone had given her leave to use his study here. She had flipped through a few books, finding several classics and a handful of her favorites but also tomes of knowledge and wisdom. Jasmine had looked over a few books but mostly kept watch on the map and the figures on the table. She had studied magic before, as all Inquisitors were given tests to see if they had any aptitude for it, but she had never found the spark in it.

The figures moved of their own accord across the map, which worried Jasmine a bit. She knew the Empire had agents outside of the Office of Inquisitors, and although Inquisitors carried the most power in office there had to be others watching her and her moves within the Empire. She was always so careful when throwing the weight of her office around; there were scores of other Inquisitors who would gladly stab her in the back to get her position. Jasmine had out-maneuvered so many other Inquisitors and other political and literal backstabbers that she had forgotten what it felt like to be safe, honestly.

So when the Emperor entered the room, without a sound, she hid her surprise when he spoke. "How are things looking, Jasmine?" the Emperor spoke in his breathless tone. Jasmine turned to see the old Elf towering over her.

"Hard to tell. It seems that Rodrigo has finally caught up with Jacques. I believe we gave him ample support in his mission." The Emperor nodded but watched the table carefully for a moment before making a face.

"It appears we put too much faith in him." Thelus pointed to the table and Jasmine watched as Rodrigo's figure seemed to crumble and fall apart. The base remained and the Emperor picked it up and set it aside. Jacques' figure continued to move toward the northern reaches.

"Damn him! Rodrigo was one of my best," Jasmine stated as she angrily crossed her arms.

"Even the best falter, Jasmine," the Emperor told her as poured himself a drink and sat in one of the chairs.

"What is your will, my Emperor?" Jasmine was hoping he did not blame her for Rodrigo's failure.

"We watch and we wait, Jasmine. Ruling has taught me that sooner or later we will be given a chance to correct our mistakes," the Emperor stated coolly as he sipped his drink.

Chapter 17-

The ship was finally about to make its way to Winter's realm. Jac stood at the front of the ship and looked north. Three mountains where in view; the smallest of the three was where Lady Winter's palace was located: Snow Peak. The second to its west was Storm's Calm, and the third to the east was simply called Omen by the gods and lesser gods who walked the world. Captain Jacob came to see the view, too.

"Been too many years since I've been up this way," he told Jac as he lit his pipe and began to smoke.

"Too enthralled raiding the Empire to come back?" Jac joked and Jacob shook his head.

"Nah, lad, Winter and I aren't exactly on the friendliest of terms," Jacob confessed as he watched the mountains closely. "We need to be careful if'n we want to get ya up to her place before she tries somethin'."

Suddenly a sharp wind rose and assaulted the ship. A fountain of ice and snow rained from the heavens to the deck. A beautiful woman stepped out of the maelstrom, wearing a dark blue dress, the color of ice at night.

"Somethin' like that." Jacob sighed deeply as they approached the woman.

"Ship *Hell-Born Corsair*, due to your crimes against the Lady Winter and her people you are given one chance to turn around and sail away, Captain Leafwind, before we rip your ship out of the sky," the emissary stated with ice in her voice. Jac stepped up to the woman and bowed deeply.

"My lady, I am Jacques Bokan. Lady Winter is expecting me, and this ship has offered to ferry me to her lands for nothing in return. In addition, several of her allies are also on board. I believe you will find that destroying this ship would come a terrible price," Jac commented before the emissary could reply. She eyed him carefully then looked past him to the distance as if someone else who was not here was speaking with her. Finally after a few tense moments she nodded and refocused her vision back to Jacques.

"You are welcomed, Jacques Bokan, but please understand that it is my duty to protect the Lady and her lands." She bowed slightly to Jac. She still outranked him in the grand scheme of things but the bow signaled that she was indeed sorry.

"It is more than understandable, my lady. I wish to give my regards to your lady as soon as we are at the palace."

"She is informed, Jacques. I will provide an escort. Captain," she said, turning her gaze to Jacob. "Follow my creatures and be wary. Any trickery or false sincerity will be met with force." Jacob nodded and bowed his head at her grimly. "Until we meet at the palace." The emissary turned back to Jac and smiled before she disappeared in a whiff of snow that flew on an unseen wind.

A flight of ice drakes came rushing through the air. The five dragon cousins screeched as they surrounded the ship. The beasts were easily twenty feet long from head to tail, with ice-blue skin of scales and massive wings. They gracefully flew through the air, matching the speed of the *Corsair* perfectly. Jac watched them closely. He had never seen drakes before and they were truly majestic creatures.

It took most of the day but they reached Winter's palace. The castle was huge, taking up most of the mountain peak and much of the mountain itself. Several tall towers were scattered about and the keep had to be fifty stories of white gleaming rock. People of all kinds and races hurried about around the castle and the furthest tower on the western side of the castle was where the *Corsair* could dock. Winter's emissary was waiting for them when they docked, and soldiers in full plate mail boarded the ship with her. They carried pikes or swords and shields baring Winter's symbol: a snowbird in flight across her mountain.

"I have been instructed to bring Jacques and Captain Leafwind to my lady; the rest of the crew and the Leafwind clan must stay on the ship until my lady says otherwise. This is not negotiable," she told them once they were face-to-face. Jacob grumbled loudly at this.

"Is all this really necessary, lass? I'm dropping Jacques off as a favor to my brother. We simply wish to turn around and get back to being wanted by the Empire," Jacob stated with a huff.

"My lady wishes you to repent for your crimes and has a task for you, one which she says you will enjoy. Our business with the Bokan family is separate to any of your prior dealings," the emissary told him, anger peeking its way into her voice. Jacob sighed deeply and motioned to the gangway.

"As ya wish, lass," Jacob gave up. He whistled and pointed at Avey, who nodded his head at him, understanding he had been given a command. They walked the halls of the castle and Jac kept a lookout. People hurried around preforming tasks, and soldiers patrolled the halls. Jac had to dodge several people to avoid colliding with them. Finally they reached Winter's throne room and it, too, was crowded. Lady Winter was meeting with various people and trying to help them with the different problems they were bring up to her court. A large, white-furred Warg guarded the door and growled at Jacob, who put his hands up defensively.

"Calm, Fenrick, I asked the, um," Lady Winter cleared her throat, "good Captain here so I may speak with him." The giant wolf stopped growling but did not back down. "If you will all be so kind as to excuse us, please," Lady Winter spoke and the room cleared as everyone respectfully bowed and left. Winter waved her hand and a table with three chairs appeared in the middle of the room, along with a flask of wine and glasses. "Please sit. I believe we all have much to discuss," she commented as she sat down. Jac and Jacob both sat as well and Winter's emissary stood behind them with Fenrick.

"I am glad to see you are well, Jacques. We had been worried for some time now," Winter told him as she poured the wine. "We received a report that the mercenaries you rode with all perished, and I also feared the worst for a time, but news of your demise did not come."

"To be fair, my lady, I do believe I had almost crossed the veil, so to speak," Jac replied, sipping the wine. It was a good and heavy wine, one that warmed his bones.

"Please do tell; it is not often we hear stories of those coming back from the dead." Winter did seem genuinely curious.

"Well, I had fought with the mercenaries and they had fallen and I managed to cut down the remaining soldiers, but I believe one of them shot me in the chest. Then I blacked out and awoke several hours later and in great pain and exhaustion. I stumbled for a bit but managed to recover." Jac retold the story and Winter listened, nodding her head.

"It's not uncommon for some important people to be revived but yours is quite different, Jacques," Winter stated and took a sip of wine before continuing. "I believe Angels came to assist you in the woods, and I may know why." Jac looked at her, puzzled, but that would fit with the dreams he had been having of Angels as of late.

"Perhaps you are correct, my lady, but I do not know or begin to understand why."

"Jacques, I believe I have a bit of a tale for you in that instance, but I have to address the matter of Captain Jacob first." Jacob was in the middle of drinking his wine and was about to spit it out when she spoke. He swallowed hard and turned his gaze to her.

"Aye, I think that would be for the best, Lady Winter," Jacob declared and Winter nodded grimly at him.

"I have a task that requires your expertise in raiding and looting—much like you have done to my lands in the past." Jacob shrugged and Jac was surprised, although he shouldn't have been.

"If that's what ya think is best, I believe I can get my crew and brothers and sister behind ya," Jacob commented.

"Well, since two of them are part of the plan so far I doubt you'll have much work to do." Lady Winter waved to her emissary, who produced a scroll and handed it to Jacob. "You'll find all the details in there about what you are doing and the results I expect from you."

"And if'n I do this, we are square, then?"

Winter smiled like a predator to prey. "It'll be as though it never happened."

Jacob tossed back the rest of his wine in one gulp before speaking. "Then, Jacques, I trust we will be seeing each other again." They shook hands and Jacob rose and bowed before Lady Winter. "I will keep you informed, my lady. Until then." He turned and walked out of the throne room.

"The captain helped me quite a bit. He pretty much pulled me from the fire," Jacques said and Lady Winter turned her head to the side.

"Helpful or not, the captain has been the cause of some trouble for my realm. While we need his services, I am willing to overlook those indiscretions," replied Winter as she sipped her wine. "But back to the matter at hand. I promised my assistance but I am afraid I require a service in exchange."

"What kind of service?"

"Nothing beyond the scope of your abilities, and perhaps you will benefit from the tasks I shall send you on." Winter poured more wine. "But you should rest; I am sure your travels have left you weary."

"I would like to speak to my mother and sister. I haven't seen them in some time now," Jac told her and Winter smiled warmly at him.

"Yes, although I am unsure of how you will talk to your mother, as she has been rather silent since her ordeal. Your sister, on the other hand, has been quite vocal about several things."

"Well, that does sound like Ioney," Jac muttered as he took another swig of wine.

Jacques walked the halls with Tegra, the emissary, who seemed quite at home with the chaos that went on in the castle. Jac was surprised that in a castle this size there were so many people about. Of course, the town was encompassed by the castle walls; although who would assault Lady Winter's castle was beyond him. Besides the fact that it was the top half of a mountain, Lady Winter could summon up a storm and make the punishing climb up the roads even worse. Jacques had heard stories of armies trying to make the climb but most were brushed off as fools' errands, although Lord Summer did once, and they had fought to a stalemate and that was how they had met and fell in love.

Jacques thought back to how he had once met their children, the twin demigods Spring and Fall, at a banquet. Spring, being the youngest by moments, was her father's daughter, quick to anger but quick to forgive. Fall was more like Winter, calm and collected but would easily and brutally defend his family and honor without a moment's hesitation. They had seemed very pleasant in their encounter and Fall was renowned speaker. Jac felt inspired when Fall gave a speech before dinner. He did wonder where they fell in the rebellion or at all, or if Lord Summer was part of what was happening. The Season Gods had been long-time allies of the Empire long before it formed, and they had supported Emperor Thelus long before he was even a ruler.

Jacques' thoughts were quieted when he entered the visitor wing of Winter's castle. Ioney was in the common room, staring out the window at the *Corsair*. She turned when the door was opened and Jac entered. She smiled brightly and tears filled her eyes. Ioney then ran to him and Jacques caught her and hugged his sister tightly.

"I thought they had captured you again! What happened, where were you?" She asked him questions in a rush of breath.

"It's a long story, Ioney, so I'll tell you later, I swear. But I want to see Mother right now." Ioney broke the hug and backed up to look at him. She now started to cry.

"You may not like what you see," Ioney told him and Jac sighed.

"I heard, but I want to see her still." Jac was firm with her and wiped her eyes. She led him to a guest room and knocked softly. After a moment of no response she opened the door and Jac walked in. It was dark in the room as the fire in the rear was low and a single candle burned at the sitting table where his mother sat. Her dark red hair had begun to gray at the crown of her head and she looked pale. "Mother?" Jacques asked when he stepped into the room. She turned toward him with cold, sad eyes. Her face was full but she had crow's feet around her eyes and few wrinkles around her mouth. This was not the same woman Jac remembered from the last time he saw her.

"Jacques? Is that really you?" She spoke with a hoarse voice, as though she hadn't used it in a long time.

"Yes, Mother, it's me, it's your little Jac," he said as he approached her. He got to his knees in front of her. She looked him over carefully.

"They said you were dead, the men at the palace. They said they had killed you. They said to give up whatever I had on them, give up all hope of ever escaping." She put her hand on his face and he nuzzled against her.

"I'm right here, Mother. It took some doing but I've come back to you." Tears started to fall from her face.

"They did things to me, Jac, horrible things. I kept screaming for them to stop, that you would kill them but they kept going..." She was crying in earnest now, and Jac rose and pulled her to him and she wept on his chest.

"I promise that nothing like this will ever happen again," Jac told her as he kissed her forehead. She looked up at him, with tear-filled eyes.

"Promise me that you will kill them. Promise me you will make them pay for everything they have done."

"I swear on Father's grave. I will kill every last one."

Chapter 18-

Ioney had explained the state of their mother when she'd arrived at Winter's castle and that she had done everything she could to try and help. They ate dinner quietly in the wing; their mother braved the bright lights of the common room to eat with them, although she didn't say much. Jac watched her closely and noticed whenever he put his hand on hers or tried talking to her, she flinched. After dinner she retired back to her room and Jac felt hollow inside. He put his cloak back on and walked the staircase to the top of the tower and looked out over the mountains.

How could his father let this happen? Jac thought to himself. He'd sided with rebels and destroyed the family. Jac even thought Harrison had been swayed by his father in this foolishness. He slammed his fist down and against the stone and regretted it almost immediately. Jacques took a deep breath and wondered, not for the first time, where Melda was. For all he knew she could have been locked up in some Empire hell-hole or, worse, shot dead and left in a ditch somewhere. Then his thoughts switched to Janna, at her home on her father's lands, finally safe from the bandits but not from the Empire. What would happen if it were found out that they had helped him?

A strong breeze picked up over the mountain and the wisp of snow flowers wafted through the air. Jac closed his eyes and let the cold wash over him. It was cold true, but refreshing all at once, and he felt as if he could live out the rest of his life here and be happy, in a manner.

Jac sighed deeply and shook the thoughts out of his head. Winter had given him tasks that must be completed if he was to ever repay her for her help or receive help in the future.

"First, I need you to climb to the top of the temple on the mountain of Storm's Calm. There you will find a family matter of yours that I require to be dealt with,

swiftly. Second, after the first I require you to travel to the coast, near Gergor's Hook. There was a fort there I allowed the Empire to build to help protect my lands, but the fort was long abandoned and now unholy creatures have take up residence and my people have made several requests that I can no longer ignore. Once these tasks are done we will speak of more I can do for you."

Jac looked out to Storm's Calm and could see a tall structure jutting up on the side of the mountain through the semi-permanent storm that assaulted the mountain with snow and ice from time to time. It is said that the storm is a reflection of the mountain—if the mountain is calm the storm is, and when the mountain is angry storm rages on. The thought of having to walk the steps of the mountain in a storm was not Jac's first thoughts for fun. Ice drakes circled the skies above him and he watched them for a time as they flew through the air gracefully. Not for the first time in Jac's life he wondered what it would be like to fly, to soar through the air without a care in the world. The jet boards did this, in a fashion, but Jac had heard stories of some mages who were able to fly with magic, for long periods of time.

Jac sighed and brushed snow off of himself and descended the stairs back to the common room. Jac hung the cloak by the fire and entered the guest room. He got ready for bed; Jac was unsure of what tomorrow was going to bring. He tossed and turned that night, dreaming of drakes, flying, and dragons soaring through the sky. He awake abruptly in the morning, having just been dreaming that a dragon had swallowed him whole. The room was cold but Jac had been sweating and he wiped the now-cold sweat from his brow and got ready. He needed to ask Lady Winter a few questions and he was not about to wait for her to see him. He flung open the door to the common room and Lady Winter was there having tea with Ioney.

"Ah, Jacques! I've been waiting for you," Winter told him with a disarming smile.

"It's very rude to keep a guest waiting, Jac," Ioney scolded him—or tried, to at least—just like always.

"I am sorry, my lady. I did not know that you were waiting for me this morning. In fact, I was hoping to speak with you as well, in private, if you'd please." Jac looked at Ioney and she made a face at him.

"I'll give Mother some tea; she always did like winter-leaf tea, after all." Ioney rose, taking the teapot and two cups with her.

"Give my regards to her, would you please, Ioney?" Winter asked with the same smile.

"Of course I will." Ioney bowed her head at Winter and knocked before entering their mother's room.

"I've grown quite found of your sister, Jacques. She is such a sweet young woman," Winter told him as he sat down.

"Yes, she can be when she's not trying to boss everyone around," Jac replied as he took a full teacup in his hands and sipped the hot liquid. The tea was strong and minty with a hint of cinnamon and white chocolate.

"I am sure you will have questions about the tasks I have sent you on," Winter stated as she sipped her own tea.

"Which member of my family is in the temple? The place looks like a ruin," Jac asked directly.

"The oldest member. Your great grandfather traveled to my realm when he was about your age. He was headstrong and impatient with the answers I gave him, and he walked to the mountain temple himself. He was gone several days and to my understanding he wrote down his adventure in the journal Ioney carries with her." *The journal!* Jac thought to himself. He had forgotten all about the small book. "But once you climb up to the temple most things will be explained, I am sure."

"Explain that my family has the blood of dragons in our veins?" Jacques asked directly again, and this caught Winter off guard.

"The short version is yes, but I am afraid you will find out there is more to it than just that." Winter sipped her tea and Jac got the impression the she would speak no more about the subject.

"Then the Emperor: why do you wish to help overthrow him?" Jacques asked. He knew why *he* wanted to but Winter was such a mystery. She thought quietly for a moment before speaking.

"Once, long ago, the Empire was everything we wanted for the world: peace, justice, order and honor. I would have marched my entire army to the gates of the thirteen Hells if the Emperor wanted it. But time began to be his downfall, and now Thelus is but a shadow of the Elf he once was."

"What do you mean?"

"Jacques, ask yourself this question: how long has the Empire existed?" That was an odd question for Jac, and he wasn't quite sure.

"Um, I believe it's existed for a few thousand years."

"And about how long does your average Elf live?"

"A thousand years, maybe two."

Winter leaned forward and looked in his eyes. "And does not strike you as odd that Thelus has lived far longer then any Elf has a right to?" Jac's mind reeled at this: Winter had a point. How had he never thought about this? It was as plain as day. "I see you understand the current problem. So the next question is, how has one Elf lived as long as he had?"

"I do not know. Magic, perhaps?" Jac answered her question with another question but he had so many more now.

"I thought the same. Perhaps Thelus has found a way. But I soon discovered it was far more sinister. That's why I am helping you, Jacques, and the others like you will be the greatest asset to the rebellion."

"What will I be?" Jac asked, more puzzled now then when he woke up.

"You'll be the hero that we need."

After his encounter with Lady Winter, Ioney helped him get ready. She handed him a long-bladed dagger.

"It'll help protect you while you are on your travels," she told him, and he hugged her forcefully then and kissed her cheek.

"I'll be back before you know it," Jacques had told her, and she smiled at him.

"You'd better be," she replied before he left the castle.

Jac had walked far past the ridge of Winter's castle and on to Storm's Calm. The path was narrow and the wind assaulted him as he tried to climb the winding mountain. Snow blew from every which way as the clouds harassed him from above. Jac tugged the cloak closer to him and even with the undershirt, over-shirt, coat, and cloak, he was still cold. Jac was just thankful he could still see in the blizzard that was coming from all around him.

After he pushed his way through a rather large snow bank, he stepped on stone, and not the dirt path from the trail. The storm broke for just a moment and he got to see the temple in earnest. The wall around the temple had crumbled for the most part and two of the three towers had collapsed and were overgrown with wild snow vines. One of the doors to the gate-house was long gone and the other was ajar and hanging on one hinge. Everything was pretty much covered in snow or ice.

Jac was about to press on when a strange feeling came over him, as if he were being watched. He pulled his pistol from its holster and pulled the hammer back; he heard it click as it locked. A pair of red menacing eyes glowed from the darkened gate-house. With a growl and a few barks, a raging Warg came charging at him. Its black fur was spattered with snow it had kicked up. Jac aimed and fired at the beast, and the bullet hit its right front shoulder and the beast whimpered but didn't stop. The creature toppled Jacques over and they both rolled around in the snow.

Jac pulled the dagger Ioney had given him and stabbed at the creature as they both slid across the ground. Its blackish-red blood sprayed across the white, perfect snow, staining and melting it together. The giant wolf howled in pain and flung Jac over its shoulder; he flew a fair distance before landing in a snow bank. He scrambled up and out of the snow before the Warg was on him again. The beast charged into the snow after him, but Jac managed to fire another shot, hitting the Warg's chest. It whimpered in pain as it collapsed in the snow. Jac put another bullet through its skull and put the evil creature out of its misery.

He trudged back through the snow and into the ruined gate-house. It was a fair-sized room; the Warg had turned into a den, and the remains of a few unlucky travelers were mixed with a pile of discarded weapons, sacks, boots, and armor pieces. There was a bed of different ripped-up and bloody clothing in the corner. Jac emptied the used cartridges from his weapon and reloaded fresh ones and cleaned his dagger on a surprisingly clean cloth hanging from a disused wagon. He said a smaller prayer to Settealla, the goddess of the dead, for the remains from the Warg, hoping that their souls would be at peace now that their killer was also dead. Jac wound his way to the opposite door and opened it easily for access into the temple itself after he took a torch from near the door and lit it with some flint.

He was greeted by a large room, where several rows of rotting pews had been untouched for some time, and an altar lay at the far side of the room. As an interior room the stained glass windows were for decoration, and each one depicted the seven gods of light in the world turned into with Settealla, and Barrin, the god of warriors and combat. The five gods of monsters and evil were clearly not present here. Jac carefully made his way through the room to the altar. A black satin cloth lay across it, and a chalice, filled with what appeared to be blood, rested on top. A black-bladed dagger was on the left-hand side and a few blood flowers lay on the right; the stems were a greenish-black color but the petals were a bright and sharp red.

Someone had turned this temple from the gods of light and order to a temple of Diros, the god of blood and vampires. Jac was not safe here.

He pulled out his pistol and turned around in the darkened room—something was here and he could feel it. Jac didn't have time to question where his extra senses were coming from. A ping from metal hitting the stone floor came from the other side of the room. Slowly, the pinging came closer and a decrepit figure came into the light. The old man was hunched over in decaying robes, and a cloth over his eyes had writing Jac didn't recognize. The man carried a metal staff with Diros' symbol at its top. The figure turned its head around as though trying to find Jac and then sniffed the air. It reeled back, disgusted, and held the staff defensively.

"Who has brought life into Diros' temple?" It spoke with a deep voice of an old man.

"Jacques Bokan, head of the family Bokan, son of James Bokan. Why have you defiled this temple?" Jac asked, watching the man closely. It smiled with a mouth of rotting fangs and laughed harshly.

"You smell like a young and foolish man, Jacques, son of James. I wonder how you taste?" The figure took a step closer and Jac pulled the hammer back on his pistol. "Hmm, what kind of weapon is that? It reeks of fire and lead," the old man asked, pausing in his advance.

Jac wondered how long had the old man been here. "It's called a firearm. A pistol, to be exact. It fires a projectile of lead with gunpowder. I can put a piece of lead through you from fifty paces." Jac said aloud menacingly, and the man turned his head to the side.

"Well, I'll have to try it once I drain the life from—" Jac fired the pistol and it pierced the man's shoulder with the bullet. The man reeled back into the shadows, screaming from pain. "Boy, you have no idea the power you are playing with! That weapon has given me pain, pain I now must give unto you." Jac heard the man run at him. He watched as he leapt at him, but Jac ducked and slammed the torch to the old man's stomach and threw him off of him. The old robes lit on fire and the old man screamed as the flames burned him. Jac fired the pistol three more times, putting two in his chest and one through his skull.

The old priest collapsed to the ground and stopped screaming and simply burned. Jac ripped the cloth off the table, sending the chalice flying and spilling the tainted blood across the floor. He tossed the cloth along with the flowers on the burning priest and felt his rage subside at the defiled temple. Jac looked around and found the open door the priest had come through and discovered it was the bottom of the last tower. Jac quickly lit a discarded torch and set it in the wall sconce. There was a coffin filled with dirt in one corner and number of old-looking books on a table with a sitting chair. The books looked unused for some-time, and Jac wondered why an old priest who had gone blind would keep books. He reloaded his pistol again as this was shaping up to be a bit more than Jac ex-pected, and he idly wondered if Winter had sent him here to clear out the present evil from the temple.

The next door led to stairs and the stairs led up, ever upward. He finally reached the top landing and it led to a door made of iron. Jac reached out and grabbed the handle and pressed down.

Locked, the damn door was locked! He thrust at the door, shaking the handle and slamming his shoulder into it. Jac soon got fed up he pulled his pistol out and was about to shoot at the lock, when he heard a *click* come from the door. He looked at it, puzzled, and pushed slightly on it and it swung open freely. Jac raised an eyebrow and kept his pistol out as he walked through the door. As soon as he was inside, the door swung closed behind him and locked. He banged at the door but turned around as the room began to light up from torches bursting in-to flames. The simply massive room was wall-to-wall in treasure, minus the small space he was standing in right now. Gold, silver, and platinum coins lay scattered all around, and swords, scepters, maces, shields, and all kinds of metal armor lay every which way.

Even with the massive pile of treasure lying at his feet, Jacques was more in-terested in the giant dragon that was curled up before him. Her scales were like polished silver and reflected the firelight brighter then any treasure Jac had ever seen. Jac was unsure how he knew that the dragon was female but she seemed to be asleep right now and Jac was not about to stand idle while a mere twenty paces from her face. He carefully stepped on the gold pile to reach for a shield when she spoke.

"Please, do not touch anything, young one. I have everything just the way I like it." She spoke in a soft voice reserved for a priestess or empress. She opened her eyes and looked at him with eyes like bright blue gems that no money on their planet could buy. Jac was going to point his pistol at her but he knew it wouldn't do anything against her armored hide. "Well, come closer, let me have a look at you." Jac swallowed hard and put his pistol back in its holster and stepped closer to her. Once he faced her, he bowed greatly as he did when meeting Lady Winter for the first time. "Come, modesty is unbecoming when in the presence of fami-ly."

"I am to understand that you are the matron of my family?" Jac asked, and she smiled softly at him.

"Of course I am, young one. In your veins runs my blood. Powerful blood at that, but I am sure you already knew that, did you not?" she asked him as she tilted her head to the side.

"I figured it out from the stories I remembered from when I was child. I had heard dragons had children with mortals, but I never thought I was one as such." Jac replied and her head moved closer to him, her chilling breath blowing on him.

"But yet you enjoy the gifts I have given you, have you not?" Jac looked at her, puzzled, and the dragon pulled her head back and snorted. Ice formed over the door behind Jac as her breath hit the door. "We were destined to meet, child. I simply made the trip easier for you." Jac thought back and remembered the warehouse door before he rescued Ioney had unlocked on its own accord as well.

"The door. You unlocked the door," Jac stated and she chuckled softly.

"Indeed, along with granting you power and skill...Well, as best as I could with us being so far apart. The blood of Judicators runs through you, child. I simply gave it a small push so you could punish the wicked."

"What about my father? Did we not share the same blood? Why couldn't you help him?" Jac asked, suddenly angry that this could have all been avoided. The dragon's smile faded rapidly.

"Your father's blood was strong but he knew from his father that his son would be the one to make things right. He did what he felt was right before he was discovered and perished. If I could have saved him I would have, but instead I had Winter come and save his family. Your father put you in a place where you would be safe from Thelus and his evils."

"How was I ever safe? I've fought tooth and nail just to get here, let alone cleaning up other people's messes along the way. Tell me how have you helped me?" The dragon's rage exploded and she leapt to her feet, forcing Jac back against the door. She swung her head so close to him that he felt as though he was being flung through an ice storm.

"I allowed your blood to awaken, and I used my powers as best as I could from as far as I was to your conflict. Did you not notice that the closer you came to me the power you wielded became stronger? No, of course not, you spoiled child! I should cast you from the heavens and push my efforts to your sister and wash my hands of you!" she screamed at him, and Jac felt frost form on his face and clothes. She stepped back and laid back down on her treasure pile with an epic thump.

Jacques stood there for a moment before finding the strength to move. He wiped the frost from his face and breathed deeply. Jac walked to the dragon and dropped to his knees and bowed his head to her.

"I am sorry, Matron, I just became suddenly aware just how much I miss my father. I am trying very hard not to squander the power you have granted me, but it just seems hopeless. I am but one man against the whole of the Empire and the Emperor Thelus himself." The dragon's expression became soft again before she spoke.

"One man has the power to change fate, to spit in the face of destiny and laugh when surrounded by danger and evil. Arise, Jacques Bokan. You are humble and brave, and worthy of the name with which I have blessed your family." Jac stood up in front of her and she smiled at him. "I have too long been trapped in this accursed place I have forgotten why I pledged to help you mortals in the first place." She rose up and stretchered her wings to their full span. "Come, I must take you to a most sacred place. Only there can your blood be fully awakened and your power be brought to its fullest."

"How will we get there, Matron?" Jac asked, a little hesitant at the answer. The dragon smiled and chuckled at him.

"We will fly, Jacques, and my name is Zada. Please call me by my chosen name," Zada told him and Jac had no time to respond as she picked him up and placed him on the back of her neck. "With the priest gone and his altar ruined, I am free to leave this place. I must thank you for that."

"Let's just call it even since you gave me the power to deal with his evil," Jac replied as he held on to the ridges on the back of her neck. She nodded her head, scaring Jac, and he held on tighter. She laughed before she breathed deeply and blew the roof off the tower and flew into the air.

Chapter 19-

Partia was walking down the hallway to the throne room; he had been summoned by Thelus rather suddenly. The minister was unsure as to why. He had sent agents into Winter's realm like the Emperor had asked. Even though Jasmine's Inquisitor had failed and died as a failure, she was still permitted to remain in her office and think of another way to capture the prodigal son of the Bokan family. His agents had yet to reach the boarder and he hoped that Lord Summer would not find out about this, or they would have bigger problems. Even with all the news entering Summer's realm being monitored closely, Partia was still surprised when Summer's emissary requested a meeting a few days ago about Bokan's treachery.

"It just comes as a surprise to my lord that a family so honored throughout the history of the Empire would turn its back on it so carelessly," the emissary had stated. He was younger half-Elf with fiery red hair and bright robes of red and orange.

"I assure you that it came as a shock to us all, but sadly the whole family was in on the plot and has since fled to the frontier and gone into hiding. I promise you that we are doing everything we can to find and bring the Bokans to justice, in the Emperor's name." This helped quell some of the emissary's questions and he left promptly after that.

"Please give the Emperor Lord Summer's regards, but I must return the Summer's lands with this news. I fear Summer will be detained for some time and wishes the Empire his best," the younger man had told him, and Partia had wondered what Summer was so busy with that he didn't come himself. Summer just loved to come into the palace like he owned the place and throw Inquisitors off the balconies. Although the man deserved his death at Summer's hands, it was still a major moral issue whenever Summer came calling.

The doors to the throne room opened and the Emperor was sitting idle on the throne, watching his glass of wine and blood carefully, as though it was to preform some feat or trick for him. Partia bowed gracefully to the Emperor who waved him off, clearly not interested.

"Tell me, Partia, why have I summoned you?" Thelus just loved his gods-damn riddles, Partia thought while wearing his best smile.

"I am unsure, my lord. I have not received any news from Winter's lands and I took care of the emissary from Summer's lands. Word is that the *Hell-Born Corsair* has sailed to the northeast, away from the Empire," Partia explained and watched as the Emperor remained seated on the throne and did not move.

"I am curious: just how far down does the Bokan's betrayal run? I honestly wish I knew. I gave the family everything they could have asked for: lands, wealth, power, protection...Was it simply not enough, did they want more? Or is it perhaps that my condition has been made public speculation?" the Emperor asked, now swirling his cup in his hand.

"I am afraid that I am unsure of that as well, my lord. Inquisitor Rodrigo had believed that the Bokan treachery was only limited to the father, but when Jacques killed several soldiers and two other Inquisitors he had a clear choice in the matter," Partia explained, hoping this would be enough for Thelus and he could leave before the Emperor's temper got the better of him.

"Hmm, isn't that the key, Ferris?" Partia hated when the Emperor used his first name, since it usually meant trouble. "Choice is what we do that defines us, is it not? Simple, easy, thoughtless choices that turn ordinary men in the great and powerful leaders of tomorrow. Was it not choice that led you to a life of service to me in my palace, Ferris, or led you to be my minister? Choices are what give a man weight." The Emperor drank from his cup, draining it. "I chose to drink all that right now, and I am beginning to question draining you and finding someone more competent to find these rebels for me. Partia, I suggest that you choose to follow my instructions and find this brewing rebellion and do it quickly before I grow hungry again." Partia did not need to be told to leave. He bowed again and walked from the throne room quickly. If Jasmine did not deliver with her Inquisitors Partia would be forced to find someone else who could.

Chapter 20-

Z ada and Jacques had flown over the northern mountains to the Patch Work plains, home of many Halfling tribes that wandered from place to place. A particularly large hill came into view and Zada landed near it.

"Here was where dragons and the mortal races of the world met. Here is where I can fully awaken your power, Jacques." Jac was half listening. He was more than ready to slide off the dragon and land on his knees. Zada chuckled at him as he dry heaved for a moment. "I take it you do not like to fly?"

"I like it fine, it's just on the back of a dragon is new for me," Jac said as he stood up leaned against Zada so he didn't collapse again.

"Come, little one, we should begin soon. I believe Winter has another task for you. One I have interest in as well." The dragon walked forward and Jac was thrust off of her and began to travel beside her.

"May I ask why you started our family?" Jacques asked, suddenly curious, and the dragon stopped to look at him. She turned her head back foreword and began to walk again.

"It was not my intention at the time, truth be told. Your ancestor, my beloved..." Zada paused as she looked to the horizon, lost in thought for a moment. "He swept me off my feet, so to speak. He was the most beautiful creature I have ever seen. Kalin was strong, fast, a true warrior for your kind, but he was also so kind and compassionate. He, of course, fought for honor and respect but was never one to boast or take more then his fair share. I was quite taken with him when we met here. I loved him like I knew I would love no other and he loved me, as well. We were happy for so long, and he had given me three beautiful children. I grieved his passing for over a thousand years, long after our children had grown and had children of their own. I tutored them as best as I could."

"Then why did you leave us? I am sure many of us could have used your advice," Jacques told her and dragon grumbled loudly.

"I tried, but then Thelus caught the ears of so many of the mortal races, and he tricked them into giving up on the power they had in their blood. He locked it away from you and yours, and all the noble families at the time had the blood of dragons or something else with power in their veins. Thelus told them that with the forming of the Empire they would no longer have need of their powers and asked them to cast it into the Eye of Stragos, a demon he had vanquished in combat long ago. Of course they did so willingly, and I was one of a few voices that warned against such action—not that any of them listened to us, of course. Thelus' words were honey to bears; after all, safety and security were hard to come by in the world at the time. I supported the forming of the Empire but not the foolishness and then simple evils that followed.

"I came to Lady Winter and asked for a place to be, and they had built a temple around me. And for a time your ancestors would come and ask for boons, which I would grant but after a time they no longer came. Then Dante came..." Zada was visibly angry at even the mention of his name. "He has been a plague to the living for some time now, hence why we are here currently." Zada pointed a wing at the hill as it came fully into view.

The hill was rather large but a stone temple had been built into the hill, and pillars of gray stone supported an archway. Strange, yet familiar, runes were inscribed on the stone and pathway of cobblestones lead to the entrance big enough for a giant, but not a dragon, to walk through. Jac wondered how Zada was going to get in but as he turned his head to look at her again, the dragon was no longer there. A radiant woman was standing near him. She had long hair of sliver strands and skin that seemed to reflect the light with eyes of bright blue diamonds and she wore a simple white dress. Jac could now see why Kalin could have so easily had fallen in love with her.

"Come, Jacques: time is an item we don't have in abundance." She lead him into the large temple and at the snap of her fingers the unused torches around the massive room lit and the room was aglow with soft light. A large bowl on a stone plinth was the only thing in the center of the room. Zada led him to the bowl and held out her hand. "The dagger Ioney has given you, and your hand, please." She smiled at him and Jac gave her both. She held his hand over the bowl and cut his right hand, spilling blood into the bowl. She spoke several words of power and the blood in the bowl began to glow with a bluish hue. Then the whole room began to glow with the same color and in a flash the room was full of blue spectral ghosts. Zada looked at one. He was tall, with long wild hair and eyes of a man who had seen much, but was still soft and kind. "My love." She spoke almost breathlessly the ghost walked to her and smiled, resting his hand against her cheek.

"Zada, you are just as beautiful as the first day I met you here." He kissed her and Jac saw a tear roll down her cheek. "Do not be sad, my love. You must be strong now more then ever." She nodded at him as she wiped the tears from her eyes. "You must be Jacques. I am proud to finally meet you," Kalin spoke as he stood in front of Jac who bowed to him. Kalin chuckled and shook his head. "You are the head of the house now, Jacques. It is us who should be bowing to you." The room full of ghosts all bowed before and rose as one. "We will begin in just a moment, but I believe someone would like a word with you." Kalin stepped away as James stepped up to Jac. He looked at his father and could hardly help the tears that formed in his eyes.

"Father, I am so sorry. I should have listened to you." The man just smiled at him, and he was exactly like Jac remembered him. His hair was short on the side and longer on top, with a trim goatee in dress clothes and a greatcoat.

"Son, please, I knew just how you would act. I would be lying if I didn't say that I hadn't acted much the same when I was your age." James laughed loudly as he patted Jac on the shoulder. "I just wanted you to become the man you are now. Make me proud, Jacques, and give my love to your mother and sister. Things will get better if you fight for it." Jac put his hand on James' and nodded at him.

"We should begin," Kalin stated as James gave his son one last smile and backed away. "Jacques Bokan, son of James, head of the Bokan family, the first Judicator in over four millennium, we grant you the power that flows in your veins; the power of the Bokan family and all the gifts it bestows to you." Kalin put his hand on Jacques' forehead and soon all the ghosts were touching him. Jac felt a wave of cold wash over him then it became a searing heat.

Jacques collapsed to his knees and screamed as he felt as if his whole body were on fire. Every inch of him burned as he writhed on the ground. Sweat poured from him and he tossed himself about as though he was covered with biting ants or other bugs were crawling under his skin. The pain was incredible and felt like at any moment he was going to succumb to the pain and die. His heart pumped rapidly and he kept grasping for breath. Finally he blacked out from the experience and sleep dulled his aches.

He awoke some time later. Zada had rested his head in her lap and was smoothing the sweat-matted hair from his face. Jac's whole body felt as though he had been thrown down a mountain. He felt things ache he had no idea he had. Zada smiled down at him when he opened his eyes.

"I was not sure when you were going to wake." Jac groaned as he sat up. "You should be careful. Your body has undergone something no one has done in a very long time, Jacques."

"The spirits are gone. I thought I saw my father," Jac whispered, a little confused Zada gave a sad nod.

"Yes. The magic to bring the dead from the veil is powerful but not long-lasting. He told me to remind you that he is proud of you and to wish your family well and give them his love." Jac nodded at her and breathed deeply. Sure, his body ached, but he felt power in his blood: true and real power. All things he had done before were mere tricks to what he knew he could do now. Jac looked at his hands, flexing his fingers and watching as the space between them glowed faintly. His eyes could pick up the smallest detail in the room even with the faint light from the torches, and he knew he could run and jump great distances with but a thought.

Jacques stood and stretched his aching muscles, which relaxed after another moment, and the pain subsided. He felt strong but he knew he was not invincible. He looked back at Zada as she rose from the stone floor. "Dante, he's my next task, correct?" Jac asked, to which she nodded her head slowly at him. "Then let's be on our way." Jac walked from the temple and Zada smiled behind him. She finally had hope for the future in her heart.

Chapter 21-

Z ada had carried him over the mountains again but this time Jac did not feel sick. He felt great. He was sure this feeling would fade with time but for right now he was riding high on the back of a dragon. A DRAGON! Jac laughed loudly as the wind whipped past him and through his hair and Janna's cloak trailed behind as he flew. Zada landed on a large cliff over looking the fort ruins. It wasn't as crumbled as Jac first thought: the walls were intact along with barracks and while one of the battlements on the fort itself had collapsed, it was otherwise in great shape. A few scattered buildings were surrounding the outside of the fort and Jac narrowed his eyes for a better look.

Skeletons patrolled the top of the walls and zombies roamed the outside along with wolves covered in fur the color of a moonless night. Jac could feel other evils roaming the ground but could not see them. "Well, no one did claim that it would be easy, that's for sure," Jac stated to Zada, who nodded her dragon head at him.

"Dante's agents were those you fought in my temple. At first I devoured them or otherwise destroyed them but they continued to come. The priest knew a trapping spell that kept me locked away while I kept them locked out of my treasure horde," Zada explained before turning back away from the ridge. "I must speak with Winter about your awakening and you must accomplish this task on your own. Speak these words to summon me and I will come and take you back to Winter," Zada spoke in Dragconic and Jac knew the words were burned forever in his memories. "Good luck, Jacques, I look forward to hearing of your success." Jac smiled and press his face against hers.

"Thank you, Zada, for everything. I'll summon as soon as I am able to." The dragon smiled at him before taking flight, winding her way around the mountains and vanishing from sight. Jac looked back, trying to figure out the best way to reach the bottom of the ridge and the opening of the fort. Jac began to wind his way down the ridge as it sloped at the edge of the of outlaying buildings. He crept across the opening between the fort, which must have been a small stable at one point, and crouched low to look around the wall. A large black wolf was sniffing the air and Jac shot back behind the building before it turned its head toward him. Jac shook his head to himself, as the wolf most likely caught his scent. He could clearly hear the paddling of its feet across the cold dirt as it came walking over to Jac's hiding spot.

Jac felt his power swell and he blinked to the roof of the old stables as the dog turned the corner and cocked its head to the side. He slowly pulled the dagger from its sheath and leapt at the beast, plunging the point into its neck. It whimpered painfully and he stabbed it several more times to quickly silence the beast. Jac then ducked through an open doorway as a group of zombies came shambling over. The smell of fresh blood and promise of meat was too much for the risen dead and they began, very loudly, to feast on the wolf's remains. Jac quickly checked to make sure his pistol and the two extra clips were loaded. He didn't want things to escalate but would be prepared when they did.

Jac climbed out of a long since busted-out window and slunk away from the pack of zombies. He wanted to blink right up on top of the fortress walls but wasn't sure where all the skeletons where and felt he couldn't go that far a distance with his magic, just yet. Jac quickly darted behind another building and climbed through the window into a former blacksmith's shop. Now his problem was the three zombies, slumped over a table, who rose as he entered the building.

"Great," was all he said to himself before rushing the zombies. He knocked one into the old forge; it fell into the fire pit and was crushed as stone from the crumbling chimney smashed into it. Jac slashed the next across the chest and slammed the dagger into the head of the last one. He ripped the dagger free and the zombie collapsed to the ground. Strangely, their eyes began to glow red and Jac felt a magical ping resonate from them. It was a warning spell!

Jac rushed over to the window and looked to the walls. Two stone gargoyles with wings, horns on their heads, and long, stony tongues and slashing claws swooped down on either side of a cloud of black mist formed. A woman stepped out from the cloud. She wore black leather armor with strips of steel molded to it, carried a bastard sword over her shoulder, and had a buckler strapped to her left arm. She didn't look anywhere in particular but scanned the whole area. He could hear her speak from here.

"We have a guest! Teach him just how welcoming we are," she commanded the gargoyles, who nodded their heads and took flight before she turned back into the black mist and disappeared. Jac did not want to wait around for the stone guardians to find him. He vanished and reappeared in the adjacent, zombie-free, building that looked like a small tavern. He saw the gargoyles smash through the roof of the blacksmith shop and then exit, each going a separate way. Jac sighed in relief as the gargoyles passed him, and he put his dagger back but pulled his pistol out. Things were about to get quite out of hand.

Jac crept out of the tavern and toward the wall, passing a group of oblivious zombies. A bakery was rather close to the wall so Jac paused in between the building and the wall. He tried to focus his new-found power, just experimenting with it for a moment. He closed his eyes and breathed deeply. He felt the wind on his face and something pass by him. He opened his eyes to find he was on the fortress walls, and three skeletons were firing arrows at him.

"Shit," Jac said aloud as he turned and fired his pistol at them. The bullet exploded on impact and scattered the skeletons every which way. "How did I do that?" Jac didn't have time to question his attempts at magic as one of the gargoyles was coming straight at him. Without thinking he pushed the gargoyle up and over his head and fired his pistol at the creature, causing the same effect, and smashed a large chuck of the gargoyle's chest to pebbles. The stone creature slid across the wall and stopped a fair distance away.

Jac heard a deep screech and looked up to see the last one coming at him now, too. Jac fired at the creature but it swooped right away from the bullet. He leapt to the roof of the bakery and rolled across it, but the wood was weak and he fell right though. Jac landed on his feet, then blinked out before gargoyle smashed into this building. Jacques began to run but the with creature's ability to fly it could easily keep up with him. The gargoyle swooped low to grab him but Jac rolled across the ground and slid on his knees and fired, hitting its back and sending it slamming into the ground.

Jacques got to his feet before more zombies came for him. He ran to the wall and did a running leap up, catching a hand-hold, thrusting him up the top of the wall and pulling himself up and over. Jac stopped to catch his breath for a moment and looked over to his left. The gargoyle he had shot in the chest was starting to move, and slowly rolled over and got to its knees.

"You must be joking." Jac said as he raised his pistol again and unleashed a blast of magic, exploding the gargoyle into rubble. Jac casually blew the smoke from the barrel. He dropped into the courtyard of the fort and took a quick look around. The main building was about fifty yards ahead of him there was a closed stable to his right and a guard post to the left. Jac opened his gun to empty the spent cartridges but something slammed against the door to the stables. Jac managed to take out the spent bullets and put back the remaining three in before the door burst open. A large warhorse from the deepest pits of the thirteen Hells was in front of him. Its hide was blacker then night, and it had fire for eyes and a mane of the same hellfire. Its tail was links of Hellish steel ending in a large morning-star mace ball. Jacques threw his arms up and made face. "What's next? Honestly, this starting to grate on my nerves." The Nightmare didn't care and snorted fire and brimstone from its nostrils.

The beast finally charged him, its hooves burning the ground it stomped on. Jac rolled out of the way and managed to doge the Nightmare's tail as it swung at him. The beast had to wheel around to charge at Jac and took this chance to fire at it. The bullet hit its chest and the demon horse reared in pain, but came coming at him nonetheless. Jac began run away, toward the stables, and jumped and rolled to his feet just before the Nightmare over took him. Jac fired again, catching it in its back leg. The beast reared again but didn't stop moving.

Jac wasn't sure what to do here. He blinked toward the stables and quickly closed the doors and barred them, hoping the beast would have the same trouble getting in as it did getting out to give him a moment to think. Much of the inside of the stable was burned and a small patch of hay remained. Something glinted in the hay from light that came from a hole near the roof of the building. The beast slammed against the doors and Jac rushed over to see what was in the hay. Skeleton remains lay here, the clothes mostly ruined. A shield was trampled and destroyed. Although there was a long sword, it was in good condition. The blade looked to be made of sliver and steel as it gleamed in the light and had a number of glowing runes on both sides of the blade. Jacques held the blade in his hand and felt his arm go numb and painful for a moment.

Who wields me? Jac heard a voice in the back of his mind.

"My name is Jacques Bokan, son of James Bokan, head of the Bokan family," Jac said aloud, not sure if whatever it was that was talking to him could hear him.

What is your purpose? the sword asked and Jac heard the Nightmare slam against the doors again, this time much harder.

"I am on a task for Lady Winter to vanquish Dante, an evil creature who inhabits this fortress."

Why should I help you?

Jac growled in anger for a moment then spoke from his heart after taking a breath. "I need to avenge the injustices brought on to my family, purge evil from the world, and bring honor to the long line of Judicators I come from." Jac spoke in the voice he knew was the calling in his blood now; not just his own voice but the voice of his family line. There was nothing from the sword for a time before Jac regained feeling in his arm.

Very well, Jacques Bokan, of the family Bokan. I grant you the power of Iskor, the avenger's blade! Power flowed from the blade and into Jacques; he knew that this blade had vanquished many evils. Jac used the power to blink back out to the courtyard. The Nightmare turned to look at him, snorting fire again before charging. Jac charged the beast as well they met in the middle of the open area. The Nightmare realized it had made a mistake, too late. Jacques slashed with Iskor across the demon horse's neck and the blow knock the beast off of its feet and sent it skidding across the ground. Liquid flames poured from its neck wound and Jac walked over and stabbed the creature through its heart. It burned to ciders quickly and was gone.

"Oh, I think you are going to come in quite handy," Jac said to the blade and he swore he heard it chuckle at him. Jac quickly reloaded his pistol before he walked to the front door and pushed the massive door open with ease. The first room was big with rounded stone pillars that held the building up. Torches were lit and a long, dirty red carpet was laid from the door to the end of the room. The woman from earlier was standing in the middle of the room; she had her hands on her hips and watched Jac carefully. She was quite lovely, but Jac could smell blood and decay on her.

"Who the Hells are you?" she asked pointedly and Jac snorted loudly.

"Straight to the point, I see," Jac stated before he bowed to her while keeping his eyes on her. "I am Jacques Bokan, and I am here to rid this land of you and your ilk," he told her, to which she laughed loudly.

"Doubtful. I am sure you will find us more than you can handle," she told him and Jac just smirked at her.

"Nothing I haven't been able to handle so far, so I apologize if I find that statement a little bit of an exaggeration," Jac told her and her smiled turned dark. "Oh, before I kill you, may I please ask your name? I'd hate to think we were killing each other anonymously."

"Please call me Jezebel, and you'll have trouble killing me when you're trapped in the dungeon," Jezebel responded and Jac raised an eyebrow at her. She raised her hand and he could feel magic underneath his feet. When her fingers snapped Jac tried to get away but it was too late: he was teleported away.

With a crack of lighting and the telltale sizzle of ozone, Jacques found himself in a cold, dark room. His head was unsteady by the magic force. Jac leaned against the wall behind him and waited for his head to clear.

Not a fan of teleporting, I see? Iskor asked him and Jac chuckled.

"To say the least, it's fine when I do it, but I get a little sick when I am thrown around against my will." Jac finally shook his head free of the fog and took a deep breath. The runes on the sword began to glow brightly, lighting up the room he was in.

This should help you see while we are down here, the sword told him and Jac nodded his head; he wasn't sure the sword could see that, or anything at all. Jac was very unsure of how the sword worked at all but he was not about to try and have an in-depth conversion with it. The room he was in was rather large, and much of it was covered in murky water. A rune was etched in the wall behind him and it looked as though someone had tried to destroy it or disrupt the magic behind it. Jac placed his hand on the wall and didn't feel any magic coming from the symbol.

"Hmm, it must only activate when the other rune is powered," Jac stated to both of them.

You must know a lot of magic, Iskor stated and Jac chuckled out loud.

"I'm pretty new at this, to be honest. I guess I am just drawing off the knowledge of the forbearers," Jac replied before he heard something splash behind him. He turned suddenly and met a pair of beady little red eyes. A rat was in the water and looked at him menacingly—well, as much as a rat could look menacingly at a person. Jac checked his pistol and it was loaded but he didn't want to waste a bullet on a rat. "Well, it's your lucky day, ratty," Jac told it as he lowered the pistol and was about to make his way across the room when a few more sets of red eyes popped up out of the dark. Then a lot more eyes appeared, and bigger ones came out, too. Several rats crept into the circle of light, and then bigger dire rats, the size of house cats or small dogs came as well.

"Well, this is *not* good," Jac stated as more and more rats came toward him. "Think I can run for it?"

Why run? Just unleash my fury! Iskor erupted with holy fire that spread like a firestorm across part of the room, wiping away countless rats and the dire rats were seared as well.

"That will surely come in handy," Jacques told him as he swung the sword around in his hand.

Sadly, I can only do that sparingly, the sword explained and Jac nodded his head as he started to make his way across the watery floor. Jac found a wooden door, which was locked. Jacques put his hand on the door and let magic flow through his hand. He could tell that not only was the door locked, it was barred on the other side. Jac slashed through the door and broke the bar in two and the door swung open. Jac pointed the pistol into the lit hallway as the door open lazily. A table with a pair of chairs was sitting in an open area at the end of the hall, and something rotting was lying on the table. Jac walked silently to the empty room.

"I heard the zapping sound. Someone got blasted down here," a voice at the other end of the hall said as Jac heard two creatures approach.

"Well, if that's the case, we should fish out the leftovers and see if there's anything good we can trade for," another voice stated. Jac looked around. The room was lit by two torches and had plenty of shadows but not enough for him to hide in, and with the evil radiating all around him, his blood called out to be let free to burn the fort down to the ground. He had to fight his instincts and he crept next to one of the torches and summoned a chilly breeze to blow the torch out. Then Jac forced the shadows to deepen and hide him effectively.

Two shambling, humanoid creatures came into view. They had sloped backs with greenish skin and wide jaws full of rotting but sharp teeth. They smelled like the dead, and had red, beady eyes along with long arms that ended with large, clawed hands. Carrions, or ghouls to most people, and Jac had heard stories of the beasts but had never seen one other than a crude drawing or painting. Thankfully they both wore ruined pants, but they covered the areas Jac was not interested in seeing on the creatures. One of the creatures looked over at the torch that Jac blew out.

"Huh, I thought we just lit that torch?" the first one asked the other who now looked over, too.

"Funny, but it's drafty down here, and with the wisps and wraiths flying around, it's bound to go out sooner or later," the second replied and the first ghoul narrowed his eyes.

"Yeah, but I just lit the torch before we left. It should keep the wisps and wraiths away till the torch started to die." There was a bag in the opposite corner Jac failed to see and the creature reached inside the bag and produced some flint. Jac tucked his pistol under his arm and quietly cocked the hammer back. As the creature reached him, Jac fired the pistol and the bullet pierced the first ghoul's chest and knocked him off his feet on to the table. Rotting meat splattered to the floor, and Jac was convinced these creatures smelled worse on the inside then the out. The second one roared and came at the shadows. Jac gracefully stepped on the table and vaulted behind the creatures, spinning, and fired his pistol, hitting the second one as it turned around to face him.

The first ghoul rolled off the table and was starting to get up but Jac pierced its skull with Iskor, and fired two more shots into the second one. He quickly reloaded the pistol and walked to the other end of the hall where the ghouls had come from. A stone spiral staircase lead upwards, Jac took the stairs carefully; the whole fort seemed to be a death trap.

The stairs lead to a large room with four square pillars. The whole room was filled with paintings and portraits of children. Different times and places, different child in each painting, and all the paintings were old. Jac felt uneasy in the room and kept turning around as though something was moving just out of his sight. Iskor glowed brightly, lighting up the room, but Jac could still not see what was moving.

"*Play with us!*" a child's voice called and Jac turned to see a spectral child run behind a pillar. Jac followed the ghost but saw nothing, and then, as he turned back into the main area, he saw three ghost girls playing with a length of rope.

"*Poor ol' Jac,*" they began to sing as one as the girl in the middle started to jump the rope. "*Lying in bed, without no blood and without a head, his blood all gone, drained by fangs, how many sips did Dante take? 1, 2, 3, 4, 5...*" the ghost girls sang, making Jac's stomach turn. He fired his pistol at the ghosts, who vanished in a puff of smoke. A number of paintings started to glow a nauseating green glow. The children in the paintings came to life and crawled out of their paintings toward him.

"Well, that's not strange at all..." Jac stated aloud as he walked slowly backwards. Their mouths were a ruin full of sharp needle-like teeth and they had cold, dead, white eyes.

"*Play with us...*" they chanted again to Jac. "*Play with us forever!*" Several of the ghosts lunged at him with clawed hands. Jac slashed at some before blinking away to another open spot closer to the wall. He didn't see the small clawed hand that grabbed his shoulder; the ghost burned his skin but did not damage his clothes. Jac blinked away again and this time saw the hands coming out the painting. He slashed the canvas, trying to hit the hands. A handful of the ghosts screamed loudly and disappeared in ghost fire. The remaining ghosts stepped backward away from Jacques, and he smiled widely.

"Who wants to play now?" he asked the ghosts before lining up a shot at another painting. He fired just as some of them came at him; the bullet ripped the canvas and a couple more ghosts disappeared. Jac slashed at the ghost still coming at him. They vanished in dark smoke but reformed elsewhere. He slashed and chopped through their ghostly forms and slashed out two more paintings as he went along. A score of ghosts disappeared being consumed by the fires of the afterlife.

Jacques turned around after he reached the far end of the wall and drew his pistol toward the center of the room but stopped suddenly. A single ghost remained in the room, an almost formless ghost.

"*Please stop.*" It spoke with the voice of countless children. "*We are forced to be here, protecting Dante's home.*" Jac regarded the ghost for a moment, waiting for it to be some kind of trick, but after nothing happened he lowered his pistol. His blood was not calling for this creature's end. "*Dante has trapped us here, the souls of lost children, for many years. We have grown bitter and spiteful with our imprisonment,*" the ghost told him and Jac felt empathetic.

"How can I help you?" he asked, honestly waiting to be ambushed but hoping it would not come to that.

"*If you destroy Dante, his power over us will fail and we will be free to join our families in the afterlife. You have the power of justice within you. You can free us once and for all.*"

"Then consider yourselves freed. Show me the way out of his room," Jacques requested, and a glowing light appeared in a painting and it swung open revealing a door behind it.

"*Please do not fail us in this task. We have waited so long for one of your kind to come and free us,*" the ghost spoke honestly as Jac made his way to the door.

"I vow you will be free before the next morning," Jac told them, bowing before he exited the room. The door led to corridor with several doors.

That was bold, Jacques, Iskor told him and Jac shrugged. *Ghosts have long memories, especially with broken promises.*

"I have already promised to destroy Dante, and it was noon when I came to the fort here. We should have plenty of time," Jac replied to the sword as he made his way down the hallway. He chose not to check any of the doors, on the chance they were booby-trapped or cursed or anything else horrible. The hallway opened up to another stairwell that led upward, but this stairwell had a large skeleton wearing armor and holding a giant broadsword standing in front of it. "Well, that is indeed something you do not see every day," Jacques spoke to the sword and the skull turned to look down at him. Jac sighed heavily before speaking. "Why am I not surprised," he said aloud before firing the pistol and piercing the skull with a bullet.

The giant skeleton swung the broadsword at Jac, who easily dodged as the creature was fairly slow. He fired two more rounds cracking the skull, which roared like wind through cavern. It was a disturbing sound. The monster swung the sword again, but with more speed this time. Jacques blocked the attack with his sword and slid across the floor from the force of the attack. Jac ducked under the massive sword and rolled past the giant before it could cut him down.

"Any ideas?" Jacques asked Iskor as he managed to avoid another attack as the giant swung his weapon overhead.

Your guess is as good as mine. I don't recall ever fighting a giant undead skeleton, Iskor told him within his mind, and Jac frowned deeply. *Although,* the sword began to muse, *most things cease to be when their heads are removed,* Iskor followed up and Jac snorted forcefully.

"Well, I guess that's a start," Jacques stated as he dodged another attack. The monster was swinging clumsily at him. "I have an idea," Jac said as the skeleton swung sideways at him and Jac ducked in time for the monster the slam its sword right into the stone wall. Rocks and masonry shot all over the floor and Jac, who barely had time to pull his cloak up over him. The giant tried to remove its sword, but it was stuck solidly in the wall. Jac rolled under its arms and blinked up to its shoulders and swung Iskor where the neck bones met just below the skull.

The blade slashed clean through the bone, sending the undead head flying from the creature's shoulders. It clattered to the floor and rolled around, gnawing at empty air. Jacques leapt down from the creature's shoulders near the skull. He aimed his pistol square at its forehead. He channeled an explosive blast, blowing the skull to pieces. The bones rapidly decayed and turned to dust and as the massive armor crumbled the bones under the weight.

"I'm glad that worked," Jacques said as he reloaded his pistol and the half-empty clip. Jac flipped the gun closed and continued up the stairs. The landing left him in the main hallway again. The front door was closed though but the torches remained lit. Jac walked cautiously from the stairs to a torch. His shoulder still burned from the ghosts touching him, and he pulled the coat open and removed his arm from the sleeve and unbuttoned a few buttons to gaze at the wound. It was blackened in the form of a small hand print.

That looks like it hurts, Iskor stated with sympathy and Jac looked puzzled to no one.

"So I must ask, can you see through my eyes or do you have your own vision? How exactly does that work? You are the first talking, living sword I've dealt with," Jac stated aloud as he began to cover up again. It was still cold and drafty in the castle.

I can see through your eyes right now. If we were to make a strong bond we could share vision. But I am mostly reserved to see through your eyes and share my wisdom with you.

"How old are you?"

I was forged by William Dragonheart, the first Dragonsmith, in centuries long since passed and faded into memory. I have found my way around the world, always in the hands of a righteous warrior. My last partner was Rufus of Beldon.

"I've heard of Rufus of Beldon. He defended Lady Winter's realm years ago," Jac said as he finished putting his coat back on. His shoulder burned, but the pain was fading slowly. He would simply have to ignore it for the time being. He rolled his shoulder, trying to dull the ache some, but it did not help. Jacques turned the corner back to the main hall and stopped at two figures, who were leaning on opposite pillars.

On the right was a man with black hair wearing hard leather armor and two sickles strapped to his back. On the left was a woman with equally black hair in a chain shirt and leathers, with a long glave next to her. They both had pale, almost white, skin and regarded him lazily with the red eyes of a predator.

"Look, Sister of Mine, our guest has joined us," the man spoke.

"Indeed he has, Brother of Mine. Jezebel said we should be on the lookout for him," Sister replied.

"She said he's been quite the troublemaker," Brother stated.

"Oh, yes, been causing all kinds of havoc," Sister replied again. "What should we do, Brother of Mine?"

"I think we should bleed him dry, Sister of Mine," Brother answered her with a smile, showing his fangs.

"Oh, yes, let us do that," Sister agreed revealing her fangs too. They turned to look at Jac, who was nodding off slightly. When he noticed they had moved he snapped his head back up.

"Oh! I apologize: are you two done? I mean, I can wait if you'd rather keep talking." Jacques rolled his eyes. Sister grabbed her glave and Brother pulled his sickles free. "So, we're fighting? I figured you wanted to bore me to death," Jac told them with a smirk. His blood was boiling just by looking at them. Sister jumped at him, raising her glave high in the air. Jac blocked the attack and threw her over his shoulder. With a snap kick, Jac slammed his foot in Brother's face as he advanced on him. Brother reeled back from the kick. Sister landed on her feet and lunged at Jac, thrusting the blade end at Jacques, who swung his sword, knocking away her blows.

He dodged an attack, spinning his right side behind him and chopping down with his sword, knocking the glave down as he elbowed Sister in the face. Brother came at him now, swinging away with both of his sickles. Jacques was a flash of steel, blocking each blow until Brother caught his sword with both sickles and pushed down on Jac, making him tumble onto his back. Brother fell on top of him, and Jac pulled up his legs and kicked him off and behind. Sister charged him with her glave, but Jac raised his pistol and fired. Sister dodged the bullet narrowly, giving Jac time to roll to his feet.

Jacques blinked behind Sister, bumping her forward and sending her to the ground. Brother now leapt at him, and Jac fired a bullet that pierced his side. Brother couldn't recover and hit the ground, sliding across the stone floor. Sister was back up, swinging wildly with her glave, and Jacques desperately swung Iskor from side to side, blocking her blows. He ducked under another wild swing and fired his pistol, catching her off-guard and hitting her right shin. She fell forward as her leg gave out under her. Brother had gotten to his feet and rushed Jac, slashing with maddening speed. Jacques used all of his focus to block the blows, wishing he would not get cut to ribbons.

Jac managed to block both sickles, locking Brother's arms down and backhanding him with the pistol. Brother stumbled away and Jac fired, but Brother juked downward, and the bullet grazed his right arm. Brother turned in time to see Jac slam his elbow into his chest, sending him spiraling away as Sister was back on him. Her glave gave her reach, keeping Jac at bay from attacking her with his sword, which was frustrating to Jacques. Finally he had an opening. He blocked a clumsy thrust with his pistol, darted in, and slashed her arm with Iskor.

Sister screamed from the pain before Jac impaled Iskor into her chest. Her scream got caught in her throat as black, thick blood gurgled up from her mouth. Jacques ripped the blade from her chest as Brother ran toward him. Jac wheeled around and cut his head off with one swift motion. The pair of sickles clattered to the ground as Brother's body fell next to Sister's and his head rolled down the hall. Jac leaned against a pillar and breathed heavily for a moment.

"Where was your help there?" Jac asked Iskor as he was catching his breath. *You were doing fine. I would have only distracted you,* the blade responded, Jac got the feeling, sarcastically. He shook his head and resumed making his way through the fort after he quickly reloaded his pistol. The main hall ended in more stairs leading ever upward. Jac sighed dramatically as he begun to climb this next set. He came to a red painted door. Jacques opened the door with ease.

The room was dark, with only a few scattered candles lighting the area. Lengths of silk hung from the ceiling and a large four-poster bed lay in the middle of room. Exotic smells wafted through Jac's nose, and suddenly his head felt hazy. He tried to shake off the fog but someone spoke before he could focus.

"Hey there, lover boy." Jacques spun around, brandishing his sword as he did. Melda was standing before him, wearing scandalously revealing nightwear. She looked as beautiful as the first night Jacques had seen her. "What's the matter, pretty boy? Cat got your tongue?" she asked playfully as she tried to approach him. Jac held the sword steady.

"I left you in Muzrun. You—you can't be here." Jac trembled as he tried to fight off the hazy feeling. She giggled her telltale giggle at him and Jac felt his heart ache. "No...no, you're not here," Jacques stated again, the haze only growing.

"But I am here, my love." Melda casually pushed his hand holding the sword away from her before she walked up to him. She put both her hands on his chest. It felt so good to have her close to him again. "I'm right where I need to be." She leaned up to kiss him but Jac shook his head and stepped back. "What's wrong, love? Do I not please you?"

"No, of course not, my love." Jac did not know where those words came from; he did love Melda, but there might be another. Just as that thought popped into his head, Jacques felt another pair of hands touch him. He turned to see Janna there, wearing nightwear similar to Melda's. She smiled widely at him.

"Well, hello again. I am so glad you found us, Jacques." Janna leaned to kiss him and Jac leaned into her.

No! Jacques, it's a trick! Jac heard Iskor shout in his mind, but the fog he was feeling had consumed him with lust. Melda had removed his pistol from his hand and tugged him to the bed.

"Come, lover, you don't need this anymore." Janna reached for Iskor but when she slipped the blade from his hands, her skin burned on contact. She yelped loudly and Jac shook his head.

"What's happening?" he asked as though he had woken from a deep sleep.

"Nothing, love. I just have a small cut from your sword," Janna told him. Jacques looked at her hand and it was clearly burned but then he blinked and saw a small cut. "I'll be fine now that you are here." They both pushed him on to the bed. Jac fell against the mound of pillows and felt completely relaxed.

"No need for this, now, is there?" Melda asked as she began to unbuckle his gun belt, and the dagger Ioney had given him rolled into his left hand. Janna had began to kiss his neck softly as Melda was unbuttoning his coat.

"My my, you are over-dressed, lover. We need to correct this," Janna murmured as she started to remove his cloak.

"This is the cloak you gave me. It has kept me safe since I left you," Jac reminded her and she smiled queerly at him.

"My love is all you need to protect you, lover. Now, let's get rid of this ratty old thing," Janna told him with a wicked grin. Jac's mind reeled at her words. She would never want him to get rid of this cloak. He opened and closed his eyes a few times and looked back at the women. They were not his loves: they had deeply pale skin, and each had a set of horns on their heads and a pair of black leathery wings on their backs. Jac clutched the dagger, pulled it from its sheath, and stabbed the monster that had pretended to be Janna. She screamed an inhuman scream with two or three voices as Jac threw the other monster off him. He ripped the dagger free and rammed it back into her again and again. The creature leapt away from him off the bed.

Jac scrambled forward, rolling off the bed to grab Iskor in his right hand. The non-wounded succubus came at him with two clawed hands. Jac slashed her across the throat and stabbed her abdomen with the dagger. He thrust the monster off of him and she fell to the floor as her corrupted blood began to pool around her. The other one was clawing her way on top of the bed.

"Dante..." She tried to speak, stuttered, then started again. "Dante...is going to end you..." Jac retrieved his belt and refastened his cloak quickly.

"Well, too bad you won't be around to see him try." Jacques sliced open her throat as well before he put his dagger back and picked up his pistol from the floor.

Who were the women you saw? Iskor asked and Jacques shook his head.

"Not the right time," he replied before continuing. He slashed through some of the hanging silk to see another door. Jac opened it was greeted by a sky full of stars. "Although it seems time has slipped away from me." He stepped on the rubble from the collapsed tower on the fort and looked out over the ruins. Somehow it had gone from around the second bell to well past the third. "I haven't been stuck in this hell-hole for that long, have I?"

I cannot tell, I am afraid. I am no more attuned to the passing of time then you are, Iskor replied and Jacques made a face.

"Oh, well, I suppose we should get a move on then, or I am going to have a small army of angry ghosts after me." Jac turned back and headed farther into the fortress' top level. He found a large locked door, and reaching out with his magic, he felt the simple lock on the door. He pressed his hand on the door and used his magic to turn the key on the other side to unlock it. This was clearly Dante's throne room. The space was small, with only a wooden throne, two torches, and two figures in this room. Jezebel stood on the right of Dante, her hand resting on his shoulder and her other arm draped over the back of the chair. Dante appeared to be only a year or so younger then Jacques. He had blonde hair and bright red eyes that looked at Jac with a mix of hatred and concern. A large hole had been ripped into the stone although the rubble was long gone.

"So, this is the up-and-coming Jacques Bokan?" Dante asked aloud before continuing. "Color me impressed...I doubted anyone could ever come this far into my lands, and yet here you are."

"Well, I guess that makes one of us. I made a few promises, and I keep my promises," Jac told him coolly as he walked up slowly.

"Hmmmm. The night is not over yet, so there is still plenty of time to kill you before the sun rises," Dante commented, leaning back in his throne.

"Please, everything you've thrown at me I have handled. Although losing all that time when I was teleported—that was a neat trick, I have to admit," Jac told him as he started to pace back and forth in front of them.

Dante wore a smirk as he chuckled softly. "Finally figured out that little piece of the puzzle, eh? Well, took longer then most, but to be fair, most have been killed before even getting that far." He placed a hand on Jezebel's, even though she didn't take her gaze off of Jacques. "Speaking of being dead, Jezebel, my love, will you kindly take our guest outside so we may throw his corpse off tower?"

"It would bring me great pleasure, my love." Jezebel turned fully toward him now, and Jac smirked and waved a finger at her.

"I don't think so, girly. Touch me and I'll cut out that shriveled dead thing you call a heart," Jacques warned her, but Jezebel did not look impressed. Her eyes glowed a dark blue and a wave of bats surrounded her, rushing Jac. He swung Iskor at her wildly but it did not stop her from picking him up and flying them out of the hole in the wall and tossing him to the roof of the fortress. Jacques blinked quickly to avoid being caught off-guard and landed swiftly on his feet, brandishing his sword and pulling his pistol free of his holster.

Jezebel landed on the roof and drew her bastard sword free of the sheath on her back. "I will destroy you!" she shouted at him before she charged. Jac blocked the first attack, then spun to his right and slashed Jezebel in the back, but her form turned to black smoke as his blade passed through her. Jezebel appeared behind him in the air, and Jac turned faster than thought and fired a bullet at her. Once again she turned to smoke and Jacques somersaulted forward as Jezebel cleaved into the ground he was just standing on.

Jac scrambled to his feet, bringing his sword up to block a slash from her. Their faces were brought close together as they both put weight behind their swords. Jac could smell the blood coming from her breath. "Do you know what I am going to do to you? I am going to rip that pretty-boy face of yours and burn it before I feed the rest of you to my wolves."

"Well, that is a mental image I will not soon be forgetting," Jac joked before laughing.

"This is not a game, you fool!" she shouted back at him.

Jac's smile turned wicked. "Good, I'd hate to think you weren't giving me your all." Jacques began summoning power into himself. The clouds overhead began to turn and twist together. His eyes glowed white and Iskor started to give off light akin to a campfire. Jac threw Jezebel off him and she disappeared again, but Jac summoned a wind and blew the smoke away, revealing her in mid teleport. She dropped to the ground and made a running charge at him.

Jacques blocked her blow and slashed her right shoulder. She cried in pain but her anger overpowered her pain. Jac rushed toward this time, slashing and chopping at her, and Jezebel had trouble keeping up with him. His assault was brutal and then Jac blinked behind her, cutting her back, then blinked again to slash at her leg, then her stomach, and then her other leg. He appeared in front of her and swiftly kicked her down. Jezebel slid across the snow on the stone, bleeding black blood from her wounds as she did.

Jacques was advancing on her when she summoned another wave of bats and tried to fly away, but Jac leapt at her fleeing form. He caught her at the top of the ruined tower and summoned a gust of brutal wind. The bats scattered every which way and Jezebel slammed back onto the stone. She scrambled quickly to her feet and tried to block Jacques' next attack, but he slashed at her hands, causing her sword to slip from her grip and fly over the edge to the ground.

Jac rammed Iskor through her heart and she gasped quietly. He slowly pushed the sword to the hilt and whispered to her. "For what it's worth, I am sorry. I know how it feels to be taken away from someone you love." Jacques pulled the sword free, and Jezebel fell from the top of the tower, blood falling from her mouth, tears from her eyes.

Jacques was taking a deep breath when he heard an absolutely inhuman roar from within the fortress. He blinked to the middle of the roof as Dante flew out of the fort. His form had changed to his true one. He was larger, with two sets of bat wings and thick, leathery gray skin and the head of bat and man mixed together.

"Well, I guess that is to be expected," Jacques said aloud, a little shocked at what Dante had turned into. The hybrid screeched after he finished; it was nothing Jac had ever heard before and he had to clutch his ears with his wrists as he was still holding Iskor and his pistol. He dropped to one knee from the absolute pain the sound was giving him. Jacques gritted his teeth and fired his pistol quickly at the creature. He fell to the ground as Dante still screamed before the bullet pierced one of his wings and he dropped from the sky for a moment.

Jacques shook his head as the pain subsided and he got to his feet. Apparently the screech wasn't to incapacitate him, but to summon the six stone gargoyles to the area. Jac grumbled as they started to swoop at him. He quickly focused his power back into him and fired a shot that scattered one of the gargoyles on impact. He leapt over the group of them, slashing one's wings, causing it to fall from the sky and hit the roof. As Jac also hit the roof he turned in place while sliding across the snow and shooting the closest gargoyle, taking its head off.

Quickly Jacques blinked into the group and slashed his way through the farthest one, leaving rubble in his wake as he landed back on the roof. He ran and used his power to grip the side of the ruined tower, climbing up with ease as the remaining two tried to follow him. They flew up and over the tower as Jac jumped off the tower roof. This was a trick, though, as he blinked behind them and fired a magic bullet that exploded in between them, scattering them to dust.

Jac landed gracefully, smirking the whole time. He turned to see the wingless gargoyle struggle to get up. He casually pointed the pistol at the stone creature and shot it to bits. Jac blew the smoke rising off the hot barrel and smiled to himself as he turned to see Dante flying at him.

The elder Vampire grabbed him and flung him up in the air, then darted after him to slam him back down. The blow connected but Jacques managed to blink to the ground and avoid the crushing force. Dante flew after him again, but Jacques fired his pistol, catching him in the chest, sending the monster reeling back. Jac caught his breath as Dante circled him overhead. The monster was fast and strong, and Jac could feel the power coming off him. He was not sure how long he could hold on to so much power.

Jacques wadded up the blood in his mouth and spit it out on ground as he watched Dante continue to circle. He knew he had one bullet left in his gun and did not want to waste the shot. Jacques would need a good clean shot to bring the beast down. If he couldn't shoot him, perhaps he could anger him enough to come and get him.

"So, I hate to admit it, but I do believe something is funny," Jac told him with a cocky smile. Dante stopped circling to face him. "You wanted Jezebel to throw my lifeless body off the roof, and yet I was the one doing the throwing. Funny how life is just full of little surprises." Jacques guffawed loudly and heartily, and Dante roared with anger but did not come flying at him. Instead he formed orbs of magical power and threw one at Jacques. He dashed forward out of the way as the orb connected with the roof and exploded, scorching the stone. Jac was darting from place to place, avoiding the blast of dark magic as Dante kept firing them at him.

Jacques, you have power! Now is the time to use it! Iskor spoke in his mind.

"You're silent this whole time, and now you decide to speak?" Jac growled at him, narrowly avoiding another blast.

You have been doing fine thus far—

"When this is said and done, we are going to have a long discussion about when to give me advice."

Jacques, do it now! the sword screamed at him, and Jac slid to a stop and took a deep breath. Lighting flashed above them and thunder rumbled through the clouds. Dante barely noticed the change as he summon a large blast of dark magic. Jac closed his eyes, letting the power he was given flow through him, picking up momentum as he began to channel the magic. Jac thrust Iskor toward the heavens, while lighting streaked across the sky and into the sword.

Dante unleashed his magical fury at Jacques with a massive blast. Jac's eyes shot open as the orb was just about to reach him. He stopped the magic power before it hit him and then pointed Iskor at him through the ball. White lighting shot out of the sword, destroying the dark magic. It streaked through the air and struck Dante. He roared as the light coursed through him, and then the heavens opened up and three more bolts struck him. The lighting sent the monster falling from the sky and he crashed through the complete tower, smashing much of the structure as he fell.

The tower collapsed in on itself, burying Dante under the debris. Jacques let go of his power and stumbled for a moment, feeling light-headed. He was sure he used too much power quickly, but minus the sudden wooziness he felt fine. He started to laugh to himself, laughing boisterously.

"Wow! I cannot believe that worked and didn't kill me."

I told you, you have power, Jacques. We should be positive that Dante is defeated before we move on.

"He's under a ton of rock. There's no way he's coming out of that." Jac pointed to the newly ruined tower, but just as he spoke he saw movement. Rocks and mortar started to shake and Dante burst up out of the wreckage. His wings were mangled and he had to be suffering from over a hundred cuts all over his body, but Dante advanced toward Jac. Jacques growled loudly out of frustration before they started to run at each other. They leaped at one another and then landed opposite each on the roof.

Jac turned to reveal the claw slashes he had across his lower left face, neck, and shoulder. Nothing life-threatening, thankfully, but they still hurt and had slashed through everything but his cloak. Dante turned to and collapsed on the roof, blood coming from a chest wound. The monster started to get back up and Jac aimed his pistol at the creature, then fired a bullet that put another hole in the monster's chest. Dante lay in the snow, breathing shallowly, as Jac walked up to him.

Jacques aimed the barrel of the gun to the monster's head. Even without any bullets Jac summoned a great burst of magical energy. Firing the blast, Dante's form turned to ash and a fateful wind picked up, scattering his remains to the corners of the realm. Jac fell to his knees and breathed heavily. He was drained and weak but he had won.

Jacques weakly spoke the words Zada had taught him, summoning her to him before he collapsed into the snow. He rolled over just as the sun broke over the mountains. He smiled in the sunlight, feeling the restless dead leave this dark place once and for all.

"*Thank you, Jacques Bokan. We will not soon forget this.*" Jac heard the wind whisper to him and he feebly nodded his head to the ghosts of the past. Zada landed after a few more moments and smiled as Jacques picked himself up off the ground.

"I see you have been successful," she stated as Jac walked up to her.

"You sound as though you doubted your kin," he replied as he climbed on her back.

"No, quite the opposite. I am overjoyed you have completed your task, as now we can begin to fight the Empire." Jac nodded to her as he yawned loudly. "Have an epic battle?"

"Indeed, perhaps I'll tell you one of these days, if either of us lives that long," Jac replied as he rested Iskor between him and Zada as to not cut him or her and holstered his pistol. "Now, if you could kindly take me back to my sister and mother, and not drop me during the flight. I need to take a bit of a nap." Jacques leaned forward on the dragon, resting his head on her neck scales. She chuckled at him, but did not say another word. He had earned his rest.

Chapter 22-

Neither Jacques nor Zada saw the small, red-tailed hawk as it landed on the hill overlooking the ruined fortress. The hawk hopped around for a moment before it transformed into a woman. She had brown hair the color of feathers, wore a cloak and scout's clothes under that. She had a headband with several red feathers in it that kept her hair out of her face. She looked over the ruins and watched the dragon land and swiftly left with Jacques Bokan.

She produced a mirror bigger then her hand but smaller then a hand mirror from her cloak and spoke with a soft, questioning voice. "Jacques has killed the Empire's agents in the area and is currently heading back to Lady Winter's castle. Should I follow?"

"*Yes, but keep your distance. I cannot afford to lose any more agents as of yet. If he leaves or more come, let me know, Aurora,*" Partia uttered through the mirror and Aurora nodded at him.

"As you command, my lord." Aurora placed the mirror back and jumped into the air, turning back into a bird in midair.

Partia sat in his study back at the capital. Aurora had been following Jacques while several of his other scouts and spies were prying into whatever Lady Winter was doing in her realm. While it would be a shame if Aurora were killed, he was prepared for that if it came to be. Partia rubbed his right temple before taking another sip of wine. Jacques was proving to be quite the handful; destroying Dante would have been no small feat. He picked up his quill again as he wrote in his private notes.

Keep a keen eye on the Bokan boy: he may prove to be just the weapon I need to dethrone the Emperor and take his power for my own.

Partia dated and signed the note before he closed his book and placed it back into the false bottom of his writing desk. Events were shaping up that could make his plans more successful then he originally thought.

Jacques awoke in his guest room at Lady Winter's castle. His body ached as though he had been through a meat grinder. He was shirtless but had on a clean pair of trousers and he swung his feet over the bed to the floor. He limped for a moment before pulling up the pant leg to see a large, ugly bruise on his right knee. Jac hobbled over to the washing stand and looked in the mirror. His right shoulder had welted from the ghostly burn but would most likely not leave a scar. Jac's left shoulder and face, however, would, and already had. There was a line just above his left jaw, one across his neck and two more across his left shoulder. They had been closed and healed but the muscles under them burned when he moved.

Jacques splashed some cold water in his face, and noticed the jar of soothing rub next to the washbasin. He was about to unscrew the top when the servant's door opened and a young maiden came in. She looked shocked that he was awake and bowed politely.

"I am sorry, my lord, I did not think you were awake yet," she told him with her head bowed still.

"It's no trouble, and please, I'm not a noble anymore. You don't have to be so polite with me," Jac told her, trying to ease her worry. She looked up at him timidly.

"But you're a hero, my lord," she stated and Jac was taken aback by this. "The monsters you slayed had been preying on towns for years, and one of those was my home, closer to the coast near the fort. There are hundreds of people in those towns who owe you a debt."

"I did it to repay my debt to your lady. If you wish to thank someone, please thank her." The maid smiled brightly but shook her head.

"No, I'd rather thank you, my lord. May I?" the maid asked, motioning toward Jacques' shoulder.

"If you would, actually. I am having some difficulties this morning," Jacques told her as she grabbed a chair.

"Here, sit." Jac did as he was told. "I have three younger brothers so I am used to applying saves." She rubbed the minty substance over his shoulders. Jac gritted his teeth from the initial sting as she touched his welted shoulder. "This looks painful." He looked over his shoulder.

He looked over his shoulder. "It hurt worse when I received the wound; now it just aches," he explained to her as the aloe began to take effect and soothe the burning. Jacques lifted his chin up as she rubbed some save on his jaw. "What's your name?"

"My name is Natasha, my lord."

"Please, my name is Jacques, but most people just call me Jac." Natasha smiled at him and nodded. When she finished, Jac looked back in the mirror at the light green rub that was over his shoulders. Then he saw the mop of hair on his head. "By any chance, are you handy with a pair of scissors?"

"Quite handy, what do you need?" Jac smirked at her.

After he dressed, with some more help from Natasha as the salve hadn't quite taken full effect yet, Jacques made his way to Winter's throne room. He wore a fresh dress shirt and pants with his boots and his newly mended greatcoat. He kept Janna's cloak back in his room but was happy to see it had been laundered and well taken care of. Winter had emptied the room except for her, Ioney, Jac's mother, and Fenrick, her white Warg. His mother smiled as he entered. Jacques had had Natasha cut his hair, leaving it short on the sides and longer on the top, much like his father.

His mother rose and hugged him tightly, and when she pulled away she moved his chin over to trace her finger along his scar on his jaw. "Well, you look very handsome, much like your father."

"I saw him, Mother. He wishes us well and sends his love." She smiled sadly at him and Jac kissed her gently on the forehead. Ioney hugged him next and kissed him on the cheek.

"This suits you, Jac," she told him with her winning smile.

"Thank you, Ioney." They hugged briefly again before they all took a seat at the table Lady Winter had had set up after Jacques bowed.

"I am happy to see you mostly unharmed, Jacques," she told him as he poured a cup of tea.

"So am I, my lady. No one declared it would be easy but then again, most things of this nature are not." Jacques joked a little and the woman giggled at him.

"When Zada came back with you in your state, we feared the worst till I had a physician have a look at you. He declared your wounds were deep but not life-threatening," Winter told him with her white smile.

"Yes, Dante was a bit tougher than I expected, to be honest, but I survived," Jacques informed, her taking a sip of tea. "I was beginning to wonder what happened to the sword I came back with."

"Ah, Iskor. I spoke with the blade after you had returned. We had much to discuss since Rufus had disappeared some time ago and I wish to know his fate and the story of you storming the fort. He was quite vocal about your exploits," Winter replied as she pet Fenrick behind the ears. "I am having the blade cleaned and sharpened for you, as well as the other boon you had asked before you left, Jacques."

"Thank you, my lady," Jacques responded with a smile, a genuine one he had not worn for some time.

"Other boon?" Ioney asked, looking puzzled at both of them.

"Some people helped me on my travels, and I wished to repay that favor." Jac explained with a look that told her he wished to speak no further on the subject. Ioney picked up the hint, as she usually did, and let the matter drop. "But now I must ask what our next move is? I have plans I wish to accomplish."

"Plans? What of your plans, Jacques?" Winter asked, watching him closely.

"I am afraid they are of a personal nature," Jac replied with a cocky smile.

Chapter 23-

Janna was walking into town; her father needed some things from the general store. Her brother, Rook, was coming home later today, and they had wanted a pie for after dinner to celebrate. She was followed closely by Galic, one of the farm hands. The tall, handsome man had dark hair and eyes. They had taken a shine to each other, even with Janna's thoughts lingering back to Jacques time and again. The night they had shared together was a beautiful experience for her, and the note he left with her vanished all doubt that if he could, he would have stayed with her.

Janna had hidden the note under a loose floorboard under her bed and tried to move on. It was dangerous for Jacques as it was: if anyone had known about their affair they both could be in serious trouble. Janna had thought it best to hide the pain of his leaving and take Galic up on his advances toward her. She prayed to the Gods nightly for Jacques' safety and perhaps one day he would return to her.

"I understand I am to do the heavy lifting, ma'am?" Galic asked, still trying to sound proper. It was enduring if not required.

"Yes, Galic, I cannot lift the flour sack I need for baking today. If you do a good job I can see about getting you invited to dinner tonight." Janna flirted with him and Galic wore a cocky smile as they walked on the main street. They turned to head toward the general store when someone called out for Janna behind them.

"Ms. Kage!" the old, high voice shouted, out of breath. They both turned to see a Gnome come running up to them. He was older with much of his hair gone, making it look like his sideburns wrapped around his head. He had a big mustache that was waxed to a point on both ends. The Gnome wore traveling clothes and carried a medical bag and several books along with a backpack that was larger than he.

"Yes, I am Janna. How may I help you?" she asked as he finished running up to her. He paused to catch his breath before responding.

"Ms. Kage, I am Professor Donald Giris, ma'am," the professor stated as he finished regaining his wind. "I am instructed to finish your medical learning if you still wish to—free of charge, of course."

Janna was shocked. to say the least. Random professors just don't show up and offer to teach for free. "Why? Who instructed you, Professor?" she asked, more puzzled than ever.

"My Lady Winter. She has given me instructions that a Ben Kaleb has provided her a service and that my teaching skills were going to be part of the payment." Janna's face flushed and Galic looked her over but didn't say anything.

"Galic, would you please take care of this for me? I'll be up to the shop in just a moment." She handed him the shopping list, and he looked at her questioningly for a moment but then simply nodded his head as he relieved her of the list. Once Galic was up the street Janna grabbed the little Gnome by the arm and dragged him off the street to between two buildings. "What do you know about Jacques? Why would he want you to come here on Lady Winter's behalf?" she demanded and the professor looked shocked and scared.

"My lady, I assure you I have no idea of what you speak. My instructions were simply to teach you if you still wish, and I have no idea who Jacques is," he told her and Janna watched him closely before she was sure he was speaking the truth.

"I am sorry, I just need to know what exactly was happening."

"Of course, Ms. Kage. These are, sadly, dark times." Donald smiled a little and nodded at her. Janna took a deep breath and smiled back.

"Have you just arrived? Do you need lodging at all?" Janna asked softly and Donald nodded his head.

"Yes, Ms. Kage, I was going to find your home once I found you on the street."

"I have a spare bedroom in my home you are more than welcome to it," Janna told him as they began to walk on the street again. A group of riders came barreling into town, making the pair stop as they rode quickly past them. The riders stopped up the street and Janna got a good look at them. Three Inquisitors and a handful of Imperial Regulars were with them, and Janna knew the Inquisitors by name.

Inquisitor Belt was leading them. The man looked unmarked by his time as an Inquisitor. He had a pleasant face with a good smile, but also had sharp, dark green eyes that cast suspicion on just about everyone he saw. His red hair was kept under his tricone hat and he wore the standard Inquisitor greatcoat. Inquisitor Smith was the next off of his horse. The older man had a big, bushy beard of wiry black and brown hair. The edge of hair around his ears was gray and his hazel eyes showed age and weariness. He carried some extra weight and his stomach carried over his shirt and was easily spotted under his coat. Inquisitor Redding was between the ages of Belt and Smith, older but not graying yet. The thin man held himself properly, and his posture was pristine and he carried himself highly above most others. His dark blonde hair was kept in a tail behind his head and he was clean-shaven.

Janna instantly felt her blood boil as she watched the men who had killed her husband stroll into town as though they owned it all. She restrained herself from going up to Belt and punching him in the face, which was doubly hard once he stopped her and smiled grimly as he began to approach her.

"Mrs. Lander—" he began but Janna cut him off.

"It's Ms. Kage now, thanks to you, Inquisitor," Janna told him coolly as she folded her arms.

"Ah, yes, my deepest sympathies for that bit of rather nasty business, but the Empire cannot tolerate rebels. Even those caught up in their web, as it were." Belt smiled again widely, and Janna felt herself ball her fists. "But as much as I would love to talk about the old times, I am afraid I am here on official business for the Empire. I am informed that one Jacques Bokan has moved through the area not too long ago. I need to know everything you have seen or heard that would be considered strange within the last couple of weeks or so."

Janna hid her shock and focused on her anger before speaking. "I haven't seen anything out of the ordinary, Inquisitor. Now, if we are finished, I have other things to do." Janna walked past him, bumping into his shoulder as she did, Professor Donald not more than two steps behind her.

"Actually, *Ms. Kage,*" the Inquisitor spoke up, stopping them. "I have heard you cared for him yourself. Your little two-horse town here doesn't have a proper doctor and I know you studied medicine at the Capital. So, needless to say, I believe we need to have another conversation in private." Belt's demeanor grew dark as he walked toward her again.

Just then a man in a dark green cloak with the hood pulled up walked past Janna, and carelessly discarded an apple core over his shoulder, hitting Belt in the back with a wet *splat.* Belt spun around, fire in his eyes, but the man didn't seem to notice as he began to eat another apple, crunching loudly.

"You there, stop!" Belt called after him, but he continued to walk. "You in the cloak, I said *halt*!" Still the man continued to walk and the other Inquisitors noticed the scene unfolding and stood next to Belt, who finally had had enough and pulled his rune blade free. "I said stop in the name of Emperor!" The man halted once he heard the ring of swords being drawn. He didn't turn but continued to eat his apple.

"Can I help you, gentlemen? And I use that term loosely, mind you." He spoke with a bit of a chuckle. The Inquisitors grew angry.

"Do you have papers? Are you a citizen of the Empire?" Belt asked with barely restrained fury.

"Yes, I have papers, but no, I am no longer a citizen of the Empire, seeing as how they want my head on a stake and whatnot," he told them before taking another bite of his apple.

"Who are you, scum?" Redding asked and the man laughed at them.

"I am sorry; my exile has tarnished my manners." He turned and bowed gracefully, the hood still obscuring his face. "I am Jacques Bokan, son of James Bokan, head of the Bokan family, and the first Judicator in hundreds of years." Janna was floored. She barely recognized his voice as he spoke. She took a step closer and saw Jac now had a scar along his left jawline. His pistol was strapped at his waist and he now had a long sword as well.

"I think we should no longer be on the street, my lady," Donald whispered to her as he gripped her wrist and gently pulled her back between the buildings. The Regulars got off their horses and came to back up the Inquisitors.

"Lay down your weapons and surrender peacefully, and I'll see that you are executed quickly," Belt told him and Jacques laughed again.

"Please, spare your words, Inquisitor. I know all about you. How you like to torture your prisoners slowly before you burn them and spread their ashes into a body of water. Also how Redding likes young girls and the ones who complain get their throats slit, while Smith has a very unnatural taste for little boys." The Inquisitors looked at each other, shaken at having their darkest secrets thrown in their faces. "You all disgust me and for that I am going to kill you, but you men," Jac pointed to the Regulars who stood uneasily among them, "you don't have to die for these pieces of filth. Simply walk away and I will spare you, but any who take up arms against me will die by my hand. This is your only chance," he proclaimed before taking another bite of his apple.

Smith's face had turned an ugly shade of scarlet as he lost his temper. "None of you will leave! Take one step away and I personally see to it that you are all executed by my hand!" he shouted at them and Jac chuckled.

"That will be rather hard to do in whatever terrible afterlife you have reserved for yourself," Jac explained, finishing his apple and tossing the core at their feet. The group looked down as the discarded fruit.

"All right, arrest him!" Redding said as he looked up, but Jacques was gone. "What in the Hells? Spread out and find him!" The soldiers looked at one another uneasily, questioning their commands.

Smith's temper exploded as he beheaded one man with a swift swing of his sword. "Traitors!" he shouted as the body hit the ground. Jac blinked before them down the street, quickly pulling out a long bladed dagger and throwing it skillfully at Smith. The blade sunk into the center of his chest and before anyone else could react Jac had pulled his pistol free and fired a bullet at the pommel of the dagger, smashing the blade through Smith's chest and caving in his ribcage.

The soldiers scrambled away as the Inquisitors turned their attentions back to Jacques. Belt rushed at Jac and swung high with his sword, but Jacques easily dodged him, sticking out his foot and sending the Inquisitor to the ground with an easy trip. Belt recovered quickly and spun around to face Jac, who backhanded him with his pistol. Blood poured out of his nose after the blow and Belt grabbed hold of his face.

"Easy, Belt, I have something special planned for you," Jacques told him before he kicked him back to the ground. Redding came up behind him and slashed him across the back, but Jac had blinked away and Redding only sliced through the after-image. Redding fell forward as Jac kicked him in the back. "Well, I suppose I should try and make this fair," he said as he holstered the gun and drew his sword free.

Janna had never seen a blade like his before. It was shiny, silver metal with glowing runes along the blade. Redding got to his feet and swung from his left, and Jac easily blocked the swing and the follow-up attack as well. He slammed his fist into Redding's face and sent him sprawling to the ground. Redding leapt to his feet and Jac dodged the quick two swings that came his way, blocked the next attack, swung quickly around, and elbowed Redding back in the face.

Janna spotted Belt getting back to his feet, but quicker than she could check. Jac had fired his pistol and pierced the Inquisitor's shoulder, sending him back to the dirt. Jacques swiftly kicked Redding while he was on the ground before turning back to Belt and regarding him.

"I thought I explained that I have something planned for you, Belt, and it would honestly be in your best interest to stay on the ground," Jac told him as he turned to see Redding get back to his feet slowly. "You've got fight in you, Redding," Jac told him as he pointed his sword at him. "It's almost too bad you're an arsehole." Redding swung wildly; Jac simply knocked it away and slashed at his left arm. Redding growled before swinging again, but Jac easily blocked the attack again and slashed at his right arm now.

Redding stumbled back a few paces and Jac watched him before taking a step forward. Unexpectedly, Redding lunged forward with his sword. Although it caught Jac off-guard he quickly recovered, dodging the clumsy thrust and impaling Redding on his own sword. Jacques slowly pushed the sword up to the hilt. Then he quickly ripped it free and swung it around, slinging the blood to the ground as Redding fell back, dead.

"And then there was one," Jac stated as he walked over to Belt. Janna came out for her hiding spot to come up next to Jacques. He looked at her with soft eyes and a smile danced at the sides of his lips.

"I'll see you burned for this, both of you!" Belt shouted as he got to his knees.

"Oh, Inquisitor Belt, you actually think you're getting out of this encounter alive? I am deeply sorry if I misled you, but you are about to die. It's just how, and I am leaving that up to Janna here," Jac told them as he looked at her and she looked back at him, confused. "Do you want to do the honors?" he asked, offering her the sword. Janna looked at the weapon and back at Belt.

"There are few things I'd like more than to see this monster dead for what he has done to me, but I cannot. I'd be no better than him if I took his life." Jac smiled lovingly at her.

"I always knew you were better than I; now I just have the proof," Jacques told her. Belt made a gamble and reached for his pistol, but Jac quickly flicked the sword and cut open his neck. Belt gargled on his blood before Jac kicked him in the chest and dropped the Inquisitor. "Murdering fuck," Jac said as he spit on the now-corpse.

"Jacques," Janna said softly and he turned back toward her. "I thought you said you could never come back?"

"I'm not back, Janna, I am here helping clear my debt to you. I've been tracking Belt and his companions for weeks. They just happened to be here while I could ambush them."

"Stay here with me, Jacques," Janna pleaded with him again and he shook his head slowly.

"I cannot, Janna. As much as I wish I could, it's not safe for me, or anyone around me. Not while the Empire is hunting me with everything they have. I'm sorry, Janna, but I am too much of a danger to you." He spoke softly as he brushed a few fingers on the side of her face. "There was somebody else I lost, before we met. I need to find her, too. I need to know what happened to her. You're better off forgetting me, Janna, but if you ever find yourself in trouble, burn this." Jacques handed her a piece of paper with a wax seal on it, a griffon flying in front of a blazing sun. "I will be alerted and do everything I can to help you."

"I don't want to forget, Jacques," Janna told him, tears at the edges of her eyes. He leaned down and kissed her softly on the forehead.

"I am sorry, truly." He smiled at her again before disappearing along with Belt's body.

"This is a disaster, Jasmine," Partia stated as they waited in one of the Palace courtyards. "Jacques has killed or scared off everyone we've sent after him. We are running out of people to send and your best Inquisitors are being killed left and right."

"This debacle is far from the Office of Inquisitor's fault alone," Jasmine barked back quickly. "Your soldiers are falling in droves whenever Jacques shows his face. If my Inquisitors had proper assistance they could have killed him by now and been done with it."

"Well, when the people they are supposed to support start cutting them up, I can't blame them for not wanting to fight for them," Partia snapped back, and Jasmine was about to launch into him when a handful of men came into the courtyard, carrying a large box.

"Sorry to interrupt, my lords, but this just arrived," a soldier stated as they set down the box. "It's addressed to Supreme Inquisitor Jasmine, and it's labeled urgent," he said as he handed her the shipping note. She quickly read that it came from somewhere north and west a little from the Capital.

"Well, open it," Jasmine told them and two men produced crowbars and popped the lid off. The body of Inquisitor Belt was in the box, with a dagger and note sticking out of his chest.

Keep sending them, and I'll keep killing them.

Love, Jacques

Partia threw up a dismissive hand as he bumped past the stunned soldiers, who were muttering to each other. Jasmine gritted her teeth with barely contained fury.

"Do not speak a word of this to anyone!" Jasmine shouted at the soldiers, who snapped out of their mutterings, bowed, and promptly left her alone. Jasmine produced a small mirror from inside her coat and brushed her hand across the front. The image flickered and changed into a different woman's face. She had a pretty face and pale, unmarked skin, although she seemed to wear a constant frown. Her golden-brown hair was barely visible under her tricone hat.

"Yes, Supreme Inquisitor? How can I be of assistance?" the mirror woman asked, bowing her head.

"Get your ass back to the Capital as quickly as you can, Katherine. I need you to head a task force I am preparing to capture Jacques Bokan," Jasmine snarled at her. Katherine's frown turned to a dark smile quickly.

"Of course, Supreme Inquisitor. I live to serve you," she stated before her image faded and disappeared. Jasmine put the mirror back into her coat and took a deep breath, calming her anger. If "Katherine the Red" couldn't bring Jacques to justice, she would have to go get him herself.

Epilogue

Muzrun was hot, even with their enchanted coats, Kesh thought to herself as she drank from a water skin she carried. She had been here for several months now and dreaded the heat every day. The desert was not the place for her—she wanted to be back in the central Empire, where the weather was cooler and the company more pleasurable. Dwarves liked to keep to themselves, and Inquisitors were frowned upon to start with. Kesh was looking for a soft young girl to curl up with. Belladonnas could supply, but they generally had their own agendas.

Kesh sighed loudly. At least the sun was setting and it had started to cool off. She took off her hat to wipe the sweat from her brow before placing her hat back and replacing the water skin in her coat. Other than the nonsense with Jacques, her station here had been uneventful. Muzrun had been in the Empire a long time and the people here did not step out of line often. Most Inquisitors would kill to be somewhere quiet and not worry if their neighbor was going to shiv them in the middle of the night. Or try to, anyway. Inquisitor training was brutal and most developed a sixth sense when it came to danger.

The third bell rang out over the desert city. Finally, Kesh thought, she could get off patrol and hang it up for the night. She wandered her way back to the Inquisitor office, always taking a different path if possible. Perhaps she could get to the pub tonight; without her uniform on she would just look like someone passing through, not a stationed Inquisitor, she mused to herself. If favors weren't owed and given she would not be stuck in this sand-covered hellhole.

"Evening, Kesh," Marta, the receptionist, smiled at her. Kesh smiled back at the young woman. Marta was quite the catch, with curly, black locks, smooth and soft-looking skin the color of almonds, and full, supple lips. Kesh let her mind wander for a just a moment before reminding herself Marta was the Head Inquisitor's daughter, and although it was not illegal, he could easy spin any story he wanted and have her beheaded by the end of the day.

"Evening, Marta. How is my lovely ray of sunshine today?" Kesh asked as she leaned on the counter.

"It's sunny just about every day here, Silver. You need something fresh," Marta told her and Kesh smirked when Marta used her pet name. Silver was nickname because of Kesh's silver tongue and ability to talk Marta into letting things slide.

"Then how about my one dark cloud, shielding me from the sun on this bright day?" Kesh shot back and Marta rolled her eyes.

"Now you're just being sappy," Marta told her with an unimpressed look. "Anyway, would you just review these papers for me quickly? The Head is unbearable right now." Marta rolled her eyes as she handed her some official-looking papers with the Imperial seal on them. Kesh made a face but took the papers. "Thank you, sweetheart."

"Yeah, uh huh, I should make you buy me a drink for this," Kesh told her as Marta made a mocking, pouting face at her.

"But who will I flirt with after the Head takes yours?" Marta asked, reaffirming the mindset that the Head Inquisitor would have her killed if he found out about her and his daughter.

"I'm sure there will be plenty of others who would line up around the block to get a chance to even speak with such a beauty." Marta blushed at this remark.

"Stop it, you, or you'll get us both into trouble. Don't you have some work to do?" Marta said, dismissing her but still watching her out of the corner of her eye. Kesh tipped her hat before walking off to her office. She opened the locked door and lit the lantern above her desk before turning away to take off her coat and hat. She stopped when she heard the hammer being pulled back from a pistol. She raised an eyebrow and turned around slowly.

"Kesh. It's good to see you, but I think we need to have a little chat," said the intruder.

Jacques Bokan was sitting in her chair, brandishing his pistol at her with his feet on her desk, smiling widely.

Acknowledgements

Wow I can hardly believe I'm here, let alone that someone is reading this. I suppose my parents were right, if you try hard enough, put in the effort and you can accomplish anything. That being said I want to thank my parents first and foremost! They told me if I wanted it, all I had to do was work toward it. So here it is, around two years later I am giving this out to the world. So Thank You Mom and Dad, I couldn't have done it with out you.

Secondly I want to thank Zoe for editing this thing, I'm sure it was not easy. Next Kyle, my good buddy for coming up with the cover art! I love it man. Morgan for reading it over before anyone else and telling me that it was confusing, which it was, which is why I changed it.

Lastly, but certainly not least, Marisa. At the time of writing this we are engaged, and I hope she'll be just as passionate with me writing when we are old and more crippled. Love you the most baby, that's it, I put it in my book, I WIN!

About the Author

When David is not writing he tends to be driving around the Galaxy or slaying dragons in far away lands. Born outside of Chicago IL, he lives with his lovely better half and hopes she will always push him to be better then he was.

www.ingramcontent.com/pod-product-compliance
Lightning Source LLC
Chambersburg PA
CBHW052001220626
47052CB00004B/1050